AMBUSH

DON'T MISS THESE
ALEX ANDER THRILLERS!

Alex Ander writes what he enjoys reading – action thrillers packed with fistfights, gunfights, good-and-decent main characters, and heart-pounding excitement and adventure...all with clean language, no graphic sex, and an undertone of faith from a Christian worldview.

Aaron Hardy – Ex-Special Forces

The Unsanctioned Patriot

American Influence

Deadly Assignment

Patriot Assassin

The Nemesis Protocol

Necessary Means

Foreign Soil

Of Patriots and Tyrants

Act of Justice

The Last Kill

Two Minutes to War

Three Days in Rome

Dark Days of the Republic

Act of War

BIG SKY Series – Sheriff Wade Lockhart

Big Sky

Ambush

Reckoning

Jacob St. Christopher – Former FBI Hostage Rescue
Protect & Defend
Word of Honor
A Vow to the Innocent
Above & Beyond
Hard Road to Redemption

Jaxon Reigns – Ex-CIA Paramilitary Operations
To Reign Supreme
Hard Reign

Special Agent Cruz – FBI Agent
Vengeance is Mine
Defense of Innocents
Plea for Justice

Jessica Devlin – U.S. Marshal
Trust Fall
No Good Options
Let the Hunt Begin

Other Action Thrillers
Kill Order
Far From Mercy
Executive One Foxtrot

FREE Ebook
Escape & Evade
Go to AlexAnderNovelist.com

AMBUSH

MODERN SHERIFF CRIME THRILLER

ALEX ANDER

This book is a work of fiction. All names, characters, places and incidents are the products of the author's imagination or are used fictitiously. Any similarities to real events or locations or actual persons, living or dead, is entirely coincidental.

TABLE OF CONTENTS

CHAPTER 1: Fresh Kill 1

CHAPTER 2: Lost in Thought 9

CHAPTER 3: Catch Me Up 23

CHAPTER 4: The Coming Reckoning 33

CHAPTER 5: Bartlett 41

CHAPTER 6: My Request 57

CHAPTER 7: All Right, All Right...65

CHAPTER 8: Your Badge 73

CHAPTER 9: Stakeout 83

CHAPTER 10: You Two Again? 97

CHAPTER 11: Closest Backup 107

CHAPTER 12: Phone Call..117

CHAPTER 13: Good Boy 127

CHAPTER 14: Old Wooden Bridge 135

CHAPTER 15: Walk Away 149

CHAPTER 16: Zest for Life 157

CHAPTER 17: Expecting Someone?.......................................167

"For I am convinced that neither death,
nor life, nor angels, nor principalities,
nor present things, nor future things,
nor powers, nor height, nor depth,
nor any other creature will be able
to separate us from the love of God
in Christ Jesus our Lord."
~ Romans Chapter 8; Verse 38-39

AMBUSH

CHAPTER 1
FRESH KILL

Partly cloudy skies had helped keep the day's warmer air from escaping too quickly, leaving the temps in the lower to middle thirties. And a three-quarter moon's rays bounced off the half-inch of wet snow that had fallen and collected on the grass and dirt beside the desolate country roadway.

Not five feet from the damp pavement, where snow-covered dirt met snow-covered grassland, two Gray Wolves—a male and a female—lay on their bellies, their snouts buried deep into the carcass of a 150-pound white-tailed deer, the pack's latest kill.

On the perimeter, four other members of the pack, their gray-and-brown coats dotted with a layer of snowflakes, lay waiting, not daring to approach until the breeding pair had had their fill.

The breeding pair went for the organ meats first—heart, liver, lungs. Once exposed, the kidneys and spleen would be next. Lastly, the muscles. Tipping the scales at more than a hundred pounds, the male would eventually devour close to twenty pounds of deer, while his lighter-weighing mate would consume up to fifteen.

With his jowls stained red, the male swallowed half a lung then licked his chops. Preparing to go back for more, he stopped to spin his head to his right, toward an arcing glow above a sharp rise in the road fifty yards away.

The female, as well as the other four pack members, all faced the same intensifying light, their heads cocked at the sound of a low, oncoming roar.

Seconds later, the roar came to a fever pitch as a pair of white lights crested the hill and lit up the scene.

The breeding pair leaped over the dead deer and trotted toward the rest of the pack. From a safe distance, with their necks cranked backward, they watched the hard-charging mechanical beast race by the dead deer before resuming their meal.

• • •

While sharp, the rise in the two-lane road wasn't enough to cause a vehicle to go airborne at posted speeds. At 90 miles per hour, however...

Sporting wide, wood-grained panels on its sides and tailgate, a boxy, old-style, hunter green Jeep Grand Wagoneer crested the incline, its tires close to three feet off the pavement. Moments later, the front wheels touched down a split-second ahead of the rear wheels. The vehicle bucked and rocked like a wild horse wanting nothing to do with the six-one, one-sixty-pound man

     AMBUSH

holding the 'reins.'

Inside the Grand Wagoneer, 45-year-old Sheriff Wade Lockhart bounced around in his seat before settling himself again. Gripping the steering wheel, his knuckles white, the windshield wipers on high, the Jeep's headlights illuminating a steady haze of fat white blotches that disappeared immediately upon impact with the warm concrete, Lockhart zoomed by the deer carcass, his mind barely registering the six wolves off to his right.

Up ahead, the road curved left. He eased off the gas pedal to veer left then right. Coming out of the second bend, he smashed the accelerator again. Taking his left hand off the wheel, he washed a palm down his face.

Wade, I-I got some bad news, Piper had told him over the phone.

Rounding another curve, he watched a truck ahead of him slow before edging to the side of the road, the strobe light atop Lockhart's Jeep reflecting off the other vehicle's back window. His right foot never letting up, he swayed into the oncoming lane, blitzed by the truck, then came back into his own lane.

Bad news.

Lockhart had heard Piper's voice crack on those words. The professional that she was, she had not been able to keep her emotions in check as she blubbered through the rest of what she had to tell him.

Coming up on a crossroad, he gave both directions a quick look before jamming his right foot onto the brake pedal while spinning the wheel to the left. When the headlights were pointing down the new road, he moved his foot back to the accelerator and straightened the wheel.

Balking at the rough treatment, the Grand Wagoneer fishtailed twice before staying true to its course.

A mile down the road, on his two o'clock, at the end of a row of trees, after another bend in the road, Lockhart could make out the parked vehicles of two sheriff's deputies. They were dark brown—almost black—Ford Explorers, and they were flanking the bumpers of an identical third Explorer. Painted with the same Big Sky County Sheriff markings as the Explorers, a four-door Dodge Ram 1500 was stationed beside an ambulance.

Lockhart took the curve to the right then mashed his foot onto the brake pedal.

The Jeep skidded sideways, its rear end swinging to its left.

Lockhart ran the gear shift to 'Park' then peeled out of the driver's seat, leaving the vehicle running and his door wide open. Wearing blue jeans, black cowboy boots, a mid-thigh black leather jacket, and a black Resistol fur cowboy hat, he strode toward the cloth-covered lump in the center of an assembly of deputies and EMTs.

Leaving the gathering, wearing blue jeans, brown cowboy boots, and a dark brown fur-collared sheriff's jacket adorned with her badge, 35-year-old, five-six, 125-

pound Undersheriff Piper Jennings hurried toward her boss while tugging down on a brown stocking cap to fight off a chill. Her straight, shoulder-length dirty blonde hair stuck out from under the cap.

Coming to within ten feet of her, Lockhart noticed puffy red bags under her blue eyes as she wiped a finger across her narrow, slightly upturned nose. When she opened her mouth to greet him, he saw a line of saliva going from her lower teeth to the noticeable gap between her two upper front teeth.

"Wade," shaking her head, she sniffed while quickly dragging a hand over her prominent chin, near the beauty mark on her right cheek, an inch from her wide-lipped mouth, "I'm so sorry." Spittle shot out of her mouth when she said the word 'so.' She pumped her hands toward him. "You're not going to want to see this."

"Out of my way, Piper."

Like a door swinging open, she pivoted counterclockwise, away from him.

Lockhart brushed by her.

She followed him. "Honestly, Wade. It's not something you..."

With his gaze squarely on the woolen blanket, he slowed before coming to a halt at the covering's edge. He dropped hands onto his hips and took several deep breaths, his cheeks puffing outward on each exhale.

Behind him, raising her arms above her head, Piper waved off the two deputies and the two EMTs.

The emergency personnel backed away and gave the sheriff space.

Reaching out to lay a hand on Lockhart's left shoulder, Piper stopped herself. She put her fist to her mouth then took a deep breath, looked away, and interlaced her fingers on top of her head, her jaw quivering ever so slightly among the crisscrossing headlight beams.

Steeling himself, Lockhart filled his lungs, took a knee, and pulled back the blanket with his left hand to expose the mangled remains of one of his deputies. He whipped his face away from the grisly sight and away from the other deputies. His breaths came in quick gasps. He put his right fist to his forehead, clenched his teeth, and fought against the tears. His hand moving to his chest, he clawed at his heart. His face twisted into an unrecognizable version of himself. He slammed shut his eyes and breathed in and out of his mouth, his lips vibrating, spittle dribbling down his chin.

Seeing his shoulders rocking, Piper covered her mouth with both hands and bent over at the waist, droplets falling from her eyes and nose.

Twenty seconds later, Lockhart covered his deceased deputy, stood, and wandered away.

Piper went after him, the hurt inside her coming through in her broken tone. "Wade."

His right hand shot upward as if he were backhanding someone.

She stopped.

He walked off the road, deeper into the darkness, his boots leaving tracks in the snow, until he was out of everyone's sight.

The deputies and the EMTs returned to the body, glimpsed Piper, then stared at the woods.

Listening, everyone gaped at where they thought the sheriff would be standing if they could have seen him. Now and then, above the quiet calm of the night, they could make out a low whimper followed by what sounded like a sharp breath.

AMBUSH

CHAPTER 2
LOST IN THOUGHT

THREE DAYS LATER
10:07 A.M.

Wade Lockhart followed Jace into the kitchen of the elder Lockhart's home. "Okay, son. What did you want to tell me?"

Jace grinned from ear to ear. "Not here. Tonight...at dinner. Let's go out...somewhere nice."

Lockhart noted his son's unusual giddiness. "All right. Sounds good. Where do you want to go?"

Jace thought for a moment. "I don't know. I'll text you later today. Oh, and," his gaze shifted toward the living room, toward his father's new friend, "you should bring Sierra, too. Something tells me she's soon to be part of the Lockhart Family."

A woman's distant voice: "Sorry for your loss."

"Well, now," Lockhart shook his head at the floor, "I've been wanting to talk to you about that." He scratched his chin. "Find out what your thoughts are on," he paused, "you know, with your mother and I—"

"Pop," said Jace, gripping his father's upper arm, "you don't have to run anything by me. I know Mom wouldn't have *wanted you to spend the rest of your life alone.”*

Lockhart smiled.

“And besides,” Jace glimpsed Sierra again before coming back to his dad, “you landed a great gal. I really like her.” He checked his watch. “I need to get going. My shift starts soon.”

A different woman’s quiet voice: “I’m so sorry for your loss.”

“Be careful out there, son.”

“Don’t worry about me, old man.” Jace slapped his father on the back and made his way toward the back door.

“Yeah, just remember this old man can still take you, punk.”

Jace laughed. “If you say so, Pop.” He raised a hand toward the living room. “Miss Courtright.”

A man’s voice: “Sorry for your loss.”

Sierra waved. “Bye, Jace.”

Jace backed out the door and was gone.

“You have my deepest condolences, Sheriff.”

Wade Lockhart blinked a few times, vaguely aware of him shaking someone’s hand. Still lost in his thoughts, he nodded at the elderly man in front of him. *John,* he thought to himself. He nodded at John, and the man moved on to acknowledging Sierra on Lockhart’s right.

Gathered on the concrete landing outside the century-old country church, the tall wooden double doors propped open on Lockhart's left, he stood between Sierra on his right and his father on his left. Funeral goers filed by, offering their condolences. The church had been full, standing room only. With most everyone in Big Sky County having voted for and known their hometown sheriff, this funeral had truly seemed like a countywide affair.

Fifty yards away, a black crow squawked.

Squinting against a rising sun, Lockhart observed the bird resting on one of the tree's barren branches. For a moment, he longed to grow wings and fly away, away from this place, this time, and the events that had come before.

"Clayton," said a man in his seventies, "I'm truly," he pumped Lockhart's father's hand, "truly sorry."

Clayton Vaughn Lockhart laid his left hand on the man's right hand. "Thank you, Ellison. And thank you for coming."

Ellison greeted Lockhart. "Sheriff Lockhart."

The two men shook hands.

"It's a damn shame. Your boy was a fine young man. A *fine* young man. Big Sky won't be the same without him."

His throat closing, Lockhart swallowed hard while whipping off a single nod.

Ellison touched the brim of his cowboy hat while

acknowledging Sierra. "Ma'am."

She smiled then bobbed her head at the gentleman.

Fighting his emotions, Lockhart spied the throng of people yet to pass then glimpsed those meandering toward the parking lot. After regarding the crow once more, he laid his right hand on Sierra's lower back. "I have to go." He stepped in front of her, descended the steps, strode toward the parking lot, and made a hard right-ninety at the sidewalk.

His head down, his strides long, he made a beeline down the walkway, his destination the fenced-in cemetery behind the church. He had almost made the snow-covered grass when a young woman cut him off.

"Sheriff Lockhart?"

He pulled up short, but his eyes and his attention were focused on headstones he could see around the back of the church.

"I'm so sorry for your loss."

He came back to her and nodded once. His soul was screaming to escape yet another 'I'm sorry for your loss,' but he stood his ground and did his best to give her his full attention.

She looked to be about twenty years old and was a petite thing, five-one at the most. She wore a tight-fitting long black dress and a white shawl under an open olive-green winter coat. The outer covering seemed too small to be zipped up over her belly bulge without breaking the zipper. Absent the heavy garb, she couldn't have weighed much over a hundred pounds.

"I knew Jace," with both eyes showing vertical streaks of mascara under them, she dragged a middle finger under her right eye, "from The Buckin Bronco. I work at the restaurant there. He," she faltered, "he used to come in, and we'd talk. He was a sweet man, Sheriff."

Lockhart nodded. "That he was."

"Well," she hesitated, "I'm sorry for stopping you. You looked like you were going somewhere." She gave him a strained smile. "I just wanted to say I'm sorry. Jace was," she cocked her head at Lockhart, "he was," her mouth hung open for a beat before she glanced down, "he was a good man. I'll miss him."

Lockhart dipped his chin again, "Thank you," then made his way toward the cemetery.

•••

Wearing a black suit, black cowboy boots, and his black Resistol hat, Lockhart stood at the back of the cemetery. The graveyard was fenced in on three sides by a white picket fence. The fourth side was open and gave way to a meadow of swaying grass. A few wildflowers of many colors—blues, purples, oranges, yellows—still poked up from the snow patches. Beyond the meadow, evergreens, and leafy trees, trees mostly void of leaves, mixed with boulder-sized rock formations on the lower slopes of a shallow knoll.

Six feet ahead of his boots sat a white marble headstone with a cross engraved in the center of its face. The top part of the headstone had 'LOCKHART' in big letters, while the lower right corner had 'Cheryl Ann,' along with her birth and death dates. Engraved flowers in the top corners and along the bottom finished off the memorial.

Facing the headstone, Lockhart shifted his attention to the plot to the left. While Jace's remains were currently in a pewter urn inside the church, with a life-sized picture of him in his sheriff's deputy uniform on a nearby easel, once his own headstone was finished, he would be buried here, next to his mother.

With his right hand inside his pants pocket, his left arm hanging down at his side, Lockhart stared at where his son would soon rest. His thoughts bounced from one memory to another, all from Jace's childhood.

Minutes later, something cold and wet struck his left palm, throwing his left arm outward at a forty-five-degree angle. He glanced down to see a 90-pound male German Shepherd turning his snout back toward Lockhart.

The 26-inches-at-the-shoulder GSD sat down on Lockhart's immediate ten o'clock, looking up at the man and displaying his broad chest. Most of the dog's face, his ears, the back of his neck, his back, sides, and tail sported black fur. His shoulders, hindquarters, legs, chest, and underbelly were a reddish, deep mahogany color, making him a black-and-red German Shepherd.

Lockhart glanced at where the animal had hit his palm before gazing into the GSD's dark amber eyes.

"That's his way of saying *Hey. What's up? I'm here.*"

Lockhart pivoted left to see Sierra ascending the gentle rise that led to his wife's—and soon to be his son's—final resting place.

At five-five and a buck-ten, 39-year-old Sierra Courtright wore a long-sleeved, below-the-knee black dress under a black overcoat. Black knee-high cowboy boots completed her simple ensemble. She sported an inverted triangle-shaped body—broad shoulders, small hips, and slender legs. With an off-center part, her medium-length, wavy blonde hair, which normally fell just below her collarbone, was up for this solemn occasion.

"You're lucky," continued Sierra. "When he wants my attention, he usually nips at the back of my calf." She half chuckled. "I lost a brand-new pair of pantyhose one time when his teeth got caught on the material." She drew up on Lockhart's left and spied her dog.

"Why is he staring at me like that?" asked Lockhart.

"Like he's always doing with me, he's now beginning to," she paused, "read *your* energy, so to speak, what you're feeling, your emotions. And since he knows you've become important to me, by extension, *you're* now important to *him*." A beat. "If I had to guess, I'd say he senses something's off with you, and he just wants to help. Shepherds are incredibly intelligent." A beat. "Also, I think him smacking your hand like that is his way of asking," Sierra laid a hand on the grieving man's shoulder, "how are you doing?"

Lockhart listed forward to touch Ranger's nose. *Not that great, buddy. Not that great.*

The dog licked the man's palm.

The sheriff gently stroked the dog's snout then went back to staring at the ground while he patted Ranger's head.

"So." Sierra squinted at Lockhart. "How *are* you doing?"

He didn't answer. He just gawked at the ground. Twenty seconds later, he stood tall, shoved his left hand into his pants pocket, and shrugged. Lifting his gaze to take in the faraway rock formations, he narrowed his eyes. "My mother died when I was nine."

Sierra cocked her head at him.

"Heart attack in her thirties. Unknown to her, she had atherosclerosis. A blood clot broke free and ended up plugging—" he shook his head, "I was at school when it happened. My father came home early from work that day and found her on the kitchen floor."

Sierra covered her mouth, grimacing underneath.

"I had gone to a friend's house after school." A tick. "On my way home afterwards, from down the road, I saw an ambulance leaving our driveway." A pulse. "Dad told me the news, and I remember not believing him. I somehow thought she was," he hesitated, "I guess I thought she was just out shopping and would be home soon."

Sierra laid her right hand back on his left shoulder.

"If I close my eyes and stay real still," he closed his eyes and tipped his head back slightly, "I can still feel the kiss she gave me...on the top of my head...as she hurried me out the door to school that day."

Seconds passed.

He opened his eyes and took a breath. "That's the last thing I remember her doing." He shook his head. "She was there in the morning and gone in the afternoon."

Sierra lowered her right arm to give him a half hug.

Lockhart jutted out his chin at where Jace would be buried. "That night at the house, when Jace pulled me into the kitchen..."

She nodded. "Uh-huh."

"...he had something he wanted to tell me, something big." Lockhart huffed. "Never seen him so excited like that before."

"What was it? What did he tell you?"

Lockhart held a shrug. "That's just it. He never said. He wanted to tell me over dinner that night." Lockhart tipped his head toward Sierra. "He wanted *you* there, too, to share in his news. He said he really liked you and that I had found a good woman."

Sierra smiled. "I liked him, too, Wade. He was always so polite to me."

Lockhart nodded to himself then returned to staring off into the distance. "Just like Mom, one moment he was there and the next moment he was gone." A beat. "And I'll never know what it was he wanted to tell me."

Sierra laid her cheek on Lockhart's left arm, her right arm coiled around his lower back, gently squeezing him.

His chest growing tighter and tighter, his throat closing again, Lockhart stiffened his spine and threw back his shoulders. "I need to go." He took off toward the wilderness beyond the cemetery.

"Wade?"

He stopped.

"Is there anything I can do for you?"

He shook his head.

"You know I'm here for you, right? If you ever need me, I'm here. You know that, right?"

"I do," he said quickly before sniffing once.

Picking up on a change in Lockhart's tone, Ranger cocked his head at the man.

"Sorry." Lockhart marched away from her and down into the meadow.

Rising to a standing position, Ranger whined then went after him.

"Ranger, heel."

The dog whirled around, came back to his owner, and sat by her left leg, both he and her looking at their departing friend.

Squatting, Sierra sat on the backs of her boots,

draped her left arm around her dog's neck, and kissed the animal on the top of his head. "There's nothing you can fix, boy." She ruffled Ranger's fur. "Sometimes, we humans just need to be alone."

Moments later, Ranger cranked his head around before letting out a low, deep, throaty growl.

Sierra glanced at him then turned to see what had gotten his hackles up. She patted his neck. "Easy, boy. It's okay. He's no threat." She faced Lockhart again.

Ranger kept his eyes on the approaching newcomer. Even though the two had formally met, they had not spent enough time together for Ranger to let his guard down.

"I hope I'm not interrupting," said Clayton Lockhart while ascending the rise. Dressed much like his son, including a black cowboy hat of his own, the 70-year-old man carried a pewter urn close to his chest.

"Not at all, Clayton," said Sierra, standing but still facing Lockhart.

Clayton Lockhart was five-ten and weighed 190 pounds. He had a pair of sky-blue eyes that matched those of his son's. Sporting thinning gray hair, he had bushy gray eyebrows, a wide bulbous nose, and chubby, sun-weathered cheeks. A well-groomed, downward-arching mustache adorned his features. Thick around his midsection, he was still tall in stature, with muscled, python-like forearms.

For decades, Clayton Vaughn Lockhart had been a

community staple in Big Sky County. His horse ranch was well known for producing some of the best animals in the area. And his charitable activities had made him beloved by many. Unfortunately, long days working on the ranch, many of them spent in the saddle, had taken a toll on his body. A few years ago, with his bones and joints protesting the cold Montana winters, he finally sold his horse ranch and moved to New Mexico.

Clayton stopped on Sierra's seven o'clock, right behind Ranger. He spied what she was spying.

"Has he always done that?" asked Sierra.

"What...head off to be by his lonesome?"

She nodded.

Still watching Lockhart, Ranger kept shooting sharp glances over his shoulder every two seconds to make sure the man back there was still behaving.

"Yeah, he's," Clayton set the urn down in front of Cheryl Lockhart's headstone, "here Jace. Keep your mum company for a few minutes, lad. I know you two are yucking it up right now in Heaven, so..." Clayton returned to stand on Sierra's right, both people eyeballing a distant Wade Lockhart. "Don't you worry about him. He may have his father's tough S.O.B. demeanor, but he's got his mother's kind and gentle heart." Clayton nodded at his son and sniffed. "Ever since he was a little squirt, he's always been a thinker. He needs to process things in his head before he can move on." He raised a corner of his mouth and let out a quick verbal click. "A trait that seemed to ramp up several notches after his mum passed."

Sierra faced Clayton. "Wade told me how she died. I'm sorry she passed so young."

"Me too, young lady. Me too."

Several moments went by as Lockhart's figure got smaller and smaller.

Sierra wrapped her arms around her lower abdomen, bent her knees, and barely hunched forward.

Clayton shot her a sideways glance to notice a grimace overtaking her features. He knew about the incident on the mountain, the one that had left her with an eight-inch gash across her belly. "Are you okay?"

"Yeah." She stood tall and breathed deeply. "It's been a long couple of days, and I'm not quite at a hundred percent yet."

He spied his watch, glimpsed his son, then came back to her. "Well, it's a good thing I drove separately. How about I take you back to Wade's place, and you can lie down?"

"Oh," she faced him, "I don't want to take you away from your grandson's funeral."

Clayton pointed at the urn. "My grandson's right there, and he's coming with, so don't you feel bad one bit. Besides," he gestured toward the meadow, "if I know my boy, he's going to be awhile."

She felt another twinge of pain and rubbed her belly. "Are you sure?"

Clayton picked up the urn, cradled it in the crook of his right elbow, then offered his other elbow to Sierra. "What kind of father would I be if I didn't see to the health and well-being of my son's lady friend?"

Sierra beamed while hooking her right arm around his elbow. "Now I see where Wade gets his gentlemanliness."

"So do I," the man winked at her, "his mother."

The two started down the hill. "Oh, I think you played a role in that too, sir."

He snickered.

"Come on, Ranger. Heel."

The dog walked beside Sierra, staying on her left side.

She retrieved her cell phone. "I'll let Wade know you're taking Jace and me back to his house."

Clayton nodded once. "Good idea."

Seated at his office desk, dressed in blue jeans and a blue denim button-up shirt, Lockhart stared at his laptop computer, his right elbow on his desk, his right hand holding his chin while he worked the keyboard with his left hand. He reversed the video then hit 'Play' again.

On the screen, a dashcam video: Jace Lockhart walked along the left side of a dark-colored sedan. Three occupants were inside the vehicle, a driver, a passenger, and a third person in the backseat.

Jace's voice: "Good evening, gentlemen. May I see your—oh shi—"

Gunshots.

An arm shot out from the driver's side.

Backing away, Jace went for his Glock.

More gunshots.

The deputy's head rocked backward a second ahead of him collapsing to the pavement, outside of the range of the dashboard camera. Only Jace's cowboy boots were visible.

The gunman fired several more times at the fallen

deputy, until the pistol's slide locked to the rear, and he retracted his arm.

His eyes as big as golf balls, the man in the backseat turned his head to look back at the deputy's patrol car.

Its tires spinning and squealing, the sedan sped away from the scene.

Minutes later, headlights appeared in the distance before a truck came to a stop. A man hurried out of the vehicle and ran toward Jace. Audio picked up cursing before the man came back into view, a cell phone to his face. "Yeah, an officer's been shot. He's hurt real bad. He's not moving." a tick. "I'm about two miles south of—"

Lockhart paused the video. *Hurt real bad*, thought the sheriff. 'Hurt real bad' didn't come close to describing the condition of Jace's body. The late deputy had been shot so many times in the head that his face was almost unrecognizable.

First on the scene, Piper had immediately known her coworker, her friend was dead. Out of respect, she had covered the body and kept deputies and EMTs from seeing Jace's remains. Then she called her boss. He could decide how best to handle things from that point.

Upon arriving, and after composing himself, Lockhart had dismissed the EMTs and instructed the deputies to process the outer perimeter of the crime scene, while he had Piper did what needed to be done with Jace's body for the official report.

 AMBUSH

Once that was completed, Lockhart and Piper had wrapped 'Jace' in two more blankets then carefully laid him in the back of Lockhart's Grand Wagoneer. No ambulance was going to transport his son. That was something he needed to do. He told Piper to say nothing of this to anyone. He didn't want people's minds conjuring grotesque images once they heard 'Jace' was shot multiple times in the face.

Lockhart then drove 'Jace' to the coroner's office where he left explicit directions that only the coroner was to see Jace's body.

Lockhart then called a funeral home to make final arrangements; furthermore, he specified that the funeral home director was to oversee the cremation process. Again, he wanted as few people as possible to see his son in this condition.

And when it came to the news media, the official statement was that Deputy Jace Lockhart had been shot and killed in the line of duty. There was no way the physical condition of Lockhart's boy was going to be sensationalized on the six o'clock news.

Lockhart rewound the dashcam footage and hit 'Play' again.

Outside his office, Piper's voice: "Here you go. One French Mocha Latte."

Bristol's voice: "Aw, you didn't have to do that. Thank you."

"Donut?"

"Any jelly-filled ones?"

"You know I wouldn't forget to get you a jelly donut."

"You're a gem, Piper. Thank you."

Lockhart banged a middle finger onto the keyboard, stopping the video, then marched out of his office.

A startled Piper spotted him. "Wade." She held a coffee in one hand and a box of donuts in the other. "I didn't know you'd be in today."

With a snarl on his face, he glanced at the coffee and donuts then came back to her.

She set the box and her drink on her desk before shedding her coat and draping it over her chair. "I can go back out and get you a coffee if you'd like."

"Catch me up on Jace's murder."

"Okay," said Piper while she shoved her tan uniform shirt tail deeper into her blue jeans. "The shooter's car was found abandoned in the woods five miles from the scene. It had been set on fire."

He nodded. "I know all that. Have the technicians found anything useful?"

She shook her head. "They've gone over every inch of it, but they said the fire must've been pretty intense. They couldn't get any prints, fibers, nothing from what was left."

"What about the car's owner? From the dashcam video, we have a make, a model, and a license plate number."

"The owner has been out of state for a week, visiting

relatives. He didn't even know his car had been stolen until I told him."

"Security cameras?"

Piper shook her head. "The owners didn't have any."

"Neighbors?"

"The guy lives out in the country. The nearest neighbor is a half a mile away."

Lockhart looked down, rubbed his chin, then lifted his head. "What about the cases Jace was working on, people he arrested, witnesses he interviewed?"

"I've gone back a month, reviewing his notes and talking with anybody he had talked to." She faced her boss and shook her head. "Nothing out of the ordinary...at least nothing I've been able to find."

"Go back another month and start all over again," a pulse, "unless that's going to cut into your," he motioned toward the box on her desk before swinging an arm toward the paper cup Bristol held, "coffee and donut runs."

Bristol recoiled.

Piper stood taller and filled her lungs.

"Now," he hooked a thumb over his shoulder, "what about that dashcam video? Where are you with that?"

The undersheriff inwardly collected herself, pushing his harsh words out of her mind. "I sent the video off to Bowie right away. They contacted me a day later and said they couldn't ID any of the men in the car. So, I—"

"Did you send it to the FBI?" barked Lockhart.

"So, I," she glimpsed the floor, making sure she measured her tone, "I sent it to the FBI. So far, they haven't gotten back to me."

"How long ago was that?"

"I sent it the same day I heard from Bowie."

Lockhart made a face. "That was three days ago. Have you called them since?"

"I made contact yesterday. They said they were backlogged, and that—"

"Call them again. Tell them a deputy was murdered. Tell them it would be great if they could get off their fat," he cursed, "and take a look at a few seconds of video." He poked his chin at her. "What else?"

Piper made a face while half turning away from him. "Honestly, Wade, there isn't a whole lot to go on. There was nothing at the crime scene. The recovered shell casings are from your standard everyday nine-millimeter boxed ammo anyone can buy in any gun store."

"Fingerprints on the brass?"

"None that matched anything in any database." A tick. "And as I said, the getaway car was torched." She faced him. "At this point, our best shot at finding out who kil—" she caught herself, "at finding out who did this, is if the FBI can get a positive ID on that guy in the backseat. Then we'd have a place to start."

Lockhart studied Piper.

She felt the heat from his hardcore stare. "I'll go back another month and start looking into Jace's reports. See if there's something there."

He glimpsed the donuts then squinted at her. "If it's not too much trouble." He turned toward his office then whirled back around. "I hired you to be my undersheriff because I *thought* you were level-headed and showed keen investigative skills."

The word 'thought' hit Piper square in the gut.

"The undersheriff is supposed to step up when the sheriff is indisposed."

Her face reddening, her chest growing warmer, Piper shot a sideways glance at the only other person within earshot of her scolding. She shifted her weight from one foot to the other while looking down at her cowboy boots.

"I expected more from you than being some, some café delivery boy." Lockhart stormed into his office and swung his right arm behind him.

The door slammed.

Piper flinched. Her head down, she held her right hand to her forehead, her other hand on her gun belt.

"Don't take it personal," said Bristol, her voice low. "He's been through a lot, more than most of us could ever imagine experiencing." A beat. "He didn't mean what he said."

Piper swallowed down her emotions. "That's what I keep telling myself, but," her chest swelled as she grimaced at the letters that spelled out 'WADE LOCKHART' on the frosted door window three feet from her nose, "but at some point," she spun right and headed for her desk, "at some point you have to wonder if what he says is true." She plopped into her chair and moved her computer mouse to activate her monitor. "Maybe I'm *not* the investigator he *thought* he hired."

• • •

One Hour Later...

"Piper," shouted Lockhart.

A startled Piper sat upright in her chair and whipped her head toward his closed office door.

"Get in here!"

She gave Bristol a wide-eyed glimpse, stood, then entered his office, her heart thumping in her chest as she peeled around the slowly opening door.

Seated behind his desk, Lockhart spied her then motioned toward his laptop. "What can you tell me about this video of Jace talking with Baxter Nash?"

Approaching from his left, Piper came around Lockhart's desk, put a hand on its surface, and hunched over to see what he was seeing.

Lockhart played the 28-second clip showing Jace stopping Big Sky County Commissioner Baxter Nash in the lounge area of The Buckin Bronco, an establishment locally known as 'The Bronc.' It was a mega complex of entertainment in Buck, Montana. The complex included a fancy, multi-floor hotel, poker and slots gambling room, pool hall, high-end strip club, restaurant, lounge bar, and horse racing track.

Piper watched the screen as Jace and Baxter had what appeared to be a normal conversation that ended up getting heated, an animated Baxter poking an index finger into Jace's chest at the tail end of the video. She pointed at the screen. "Yeah, I tried to speak with Commissioner Nash, but he froze me out."

"What do you mean?"

"I mean, I called his office and asked if I could speak with him. I heard nothing from either him or his secretary, so I kept calling. Finally, after the fourth or fifth call, his secretary got all pissy with me, told me to stop calling, and hung up."

"What did you do?"

"Well," Piper tweaked her neck, "no snarky little witch is going to talk to me that way, so I paid Commissioner Nash a visit."

"And?"

"And that's when he dodged my questions, telling me if I knew what was best for my career, that I should quit while I was ahead." She shrugged. "I really had nothing official to go on, Wade, except for," she motioned toward the video, "this. And the last time I checked; conversations weren't illegal. So, there was no way I could press him any further. I knew going in that," a pulse, "whatever he told me was going to have to be offered in good faith." She huffed. "And he wasn't in a faith-filled mood."

Lockhart stood, yanked his leather jacket from off his chair, did an end run around her, and headed toward the open office door.

Piper stood tall. "Where are you going?"

"Baxter might not have been willing to talk to *you*, but he's damn well going to talk to *me*."

CHAPTER 4
THE COMING RECKONING

Lockhart had made the five-minute walk down Main Street to the Big Sky County Building, ascended the steps to the second floor, and was now standing in front of the main desk, an older lady with graying, curly hair and narrow wire-rimmed glasses staring up at him. "I need to see Baxter Nash."

"I'm sorry, Sheriff, but he doesn't want to be disturbed at th—"

Lockhart stepped away, "It's important," and marched toward Baxter's closed office door.

"You can't go in there," said the receptionist, chasing after him with an outstretched arm.

He threw open the door and barged into the office.

Behind his desk, sitting in a high-back leather chair, Baxter whirled around at the intrusion, several sheets of paper in his hands.

"We need to talk," said Lockhart.

"Sir," said the receptionist, "I told him you didn't want to be disturbed."

"What were you and my son talking about at the Bronc?"

Her arms crossed, her lips puckered, the receptionist fumed while eyeing Lockhart.

Baxter got her attention and motioned toward the door. "I'll handle this, Vera."

After sending the sheriff a few more visual daggers, she left the office and closed the door.

The office was decorated with black leather chairs, Queen Anne tables, bookcases, and footstools. Cream-colored shag carpeting, brown curtains, and frosted glass floor lamps rounded out the décor. The lamps created a warm, homey atmosphere with the harsh overhead lighting off.

Lockhart weaved his way between the two straight-back chairs facing Baxter's desk and stopped. "You're on video having a conversation with Jace two days before he was killed. It didn't appear to be an amicable conversation. I want to know what you two were talking about?"

Baxter huffed while half smiling. "Wade," he laid his paperwork on top of other papers strewn around the desk, "I don't owe you any explanation on what your son and I were discussing." Dressed in a Circle S Boise Heather Brown Western suit coat and matching dress ranch pants—the coat having decorative, suede-look front and back yokes with inverted arrow detailing—he leaned back in his chair while adjusting his black tie and the cuffs on his white dress shirt. Resting elbows on the chair's arm and steepling his fingers, he crossed his legs, ankle on knee, to display black-and-brown crocodile cowboy boots. "Unless, of course," he spread his splayed fingers apart a foot, "private conversations between citizens are somehow now illegal in this county."

Glaring at Baxter, Lockhart recalled his undersheriff saying much the same thing.

"But," continued Baxter, "if you absolutely must know," a beat, "your son offered me his condolences on the death of *my* sons." He cocked his head an inch to the side. "You remember Dallas and Dawson, don't you, Wade?"

Lockhart and Baxter's thirty-year relationship was complicated at best. The two had competed in high school football—Lockhart, a wide receiver; Nash, a defensive back—several times. They had also vied for first place at youth rodeos, often exchanging one-two finishes in calf roping and steer wrestling.

During Lockhart's first bid for sheriff, Baxter had also run for the office. And Baxter had lost, the voters preferring Lockhart's morals and the fact that he was a hometown 'Big Sky boy' who had made good.

More recently, the Lockhart-Baxter feud had taken a dark turn, with Lockhart having executed a raid on a cabin in the mountains to rescue a kidnapped young woman. He had shot and killed Dallas Nash while Sierra Courtright had killed the man's brother Dawson to save her dog Ranger from being stabbed to death.

"By the way," continued Baxter, "I don't recall seeing

you at the funeral."

"Didn't think my attendance would have been in the best interest of those present."

Baxter half laughed. "No, I don't suppose it would have been."

Moments passed.

Lockhart shifted his weight. "From what I saw in that video, you seemed upset with Jace."

"I was. He offered his condolences, and I told him to go," Baxter let loose with a vulgar term, "himself."

Lockhart's brows went higher.

"I didn't need or want your son's pity." A tick. "And while you're here, I'll tell you the same thing. Go," he thrust out an index finger toward the sheriff and repeated the same vulgarity, "*your*self." Two pulses. "You took my family from me, and I'll *never* forget that. And now that you've lost your boy, may you never know peace again for as long as you live."

Lockhart bristled, his muscles tensing. "Different circumstances, Bax. Your boys had killed one woman and kidnapped another. They were breaking the law, and I was only—"

"Exacting your revenge against," Baxter shot to his feet and jabbed his thumb into his chest, "*me*. Only you chose to take your pound of flesh from my boys." He stabbed at the air between him and the lawman. "*That's* what you were doing. There were a lot of other ways you could've handled that situation." Baxter pushed his chair

     AMBUSH

away with the backs of his knees and charged around the desk. Nose to nose, the 45-year-old, six-foot, one-eighty-five-pound county commissioner confronted his nemesis. "But no. You had to go in hard and fast," he threw up an arm, "with your guns a blazing like you were some, some, some old-time sheriff from the wild West."

Listing forward, Lockhart growled, "If I *hadn't* acted, that young girl would've been—" he pulled away. Logic and reasoning would not work on Baxter. The man was blinded by rage. Lockhart knew all too well what anger did to one's mental processes. He was currently battling his own demons, struggling to maintain his own sanity when nothing around him made sense.

Lockhart backed away from the man while trying to calm himself. He made it a point to keep his voice steady and low. "If you recall anything that could help in finding the men who murdered Jace, I'd appreciate a call." He turned around.

"Don't hold your breath, Sheriff."

Lockhart opened the door and left the office, leaving the door open.

Baxter raised his voice. "Mark my words, Wade. There's a *reckoning* coming for men like us."

• • •

Five Minutes Later...
Back at the Big Sky Sheriff's office, Lockhart strode

past Bristol on his right. The woman was on a phone call with a citizen.

Standing at her desk, hunched over her printer, Piper snatched a sheet of paper before it hit the tray. "Wade, I got it." She met him as he made the left turn toward his office. "I got it. I kept calling my contact over at the FBI. Didn't stop pressing him until he caved." She closed one eye and bobbed her head from side to side. "Pretty sure we've burned our bridges with Agent Wilkins, but it was worth it." She held up the paper. "He had someone process the dashcam footage, and they got a hit right away, a 75-percent match."

Lockhart plucked the paper from her hand, skimmed the information, then did a one-eighty to march toward the saloon doors he had just passed through, doors that separated the main lobby from administration.

Piper grabbed her jacket, twirled it around her shoulders, and slid arms into sleeves. Flipping her hair out, she caught up to him.

"Where do you think you're going?" he said.

"With you."

"Nope. I'm working this lead alone."

She picked up her pace and spun left to intercept him, her back a foot from the swinging doors, Bristol on her two o'clock. "Not this time."

He leaned away from her, his eyebrows rising higher.

"With all due respect, your head isn't screwed on tight at the moment."

Her eyes wide, Bristol went from one person to the other. "Please hold," she said, tapping her headset a beat later.

"I get it," continued Piper. "You're going through a lot. You've been through a lot. Life is crap right now. But I'll be danged if I'm going to let you walk out that door without having at least *tried* to keep you from doing something stupid, something you might end up regretting, something that might end up costing you your job," a tick, "or worse yet, your freedom." She made a show of crossing her arms over her chest and throwing out her right hip. "So, either fire my," she cursed, "or," then bobbed her head backward, "let's get on the road."

Her heart rate rising, Bristol kept shooting alternating glances at the twosome.

Lockhart gaped at his undersheriff. Not long ago, he had been ripping her a 'new one,' all the while knowing he was wrong. It was as if he had been having an out-of-body experience, and he had no control over what he had been saying. Piper had done everything by the book regarding Jace's murder investigation. He had no right to chew her out like he had done. He wasn't himself. His son's murder case was no closer to being solved today than it had been five days ago. He was hurting. He was angry. And poor Piper had just happened to be in his way when he had pulled the trigger on the proverbial shotgun. And now here she was, risking her job to save him from possibly losing *his* job...or something *worse*, as she had put it.

Piper's heart was in her throat. Her armpits were damp. Her face was flushed.

Lockhart and his second-in-command exchanged stoic looks. A second later, he veered right and brushed by her, "*You* drive," before entering the main lobby.

Piper let out a long breath, her deflating chest shaking as she exhaled. She held out twitching hands, flexing her fingers while giving Bristol a 'I can't believe I just did that' look.

Bristol smiled. "Atta girl." She tipped her head toward the departing Lockhart, spying him through the glass windows that ran from a short wall to the ceiling. "He may not know it, but he needs you. Go. Look after him."

Piper nodded and backed through the saloon doors while fishing her truck keys from a jean pocket.

CHAPTER 5
BARTLETT

The Big Sky County four-door Dodge Ram 1500 SSV (Special Service Vehicle) cruised south on I-15, five miles per hour above posted speed limits. If Lockhart had been driving, that number would have been higher. But with Piper behind the wheel, she ensured they would not draw unwanted—and time-consuming—attention from state troopers patrolling the interstate.

Lockhart perused the information on Roger E. Bartlett, a 31-year-old repeat offender with a criminal record of mostly petty thefts, save one count of taking part in a bank robbery. Barlett had been the 'wheelman' during that heist. He eventually gave up his accomplices for a reduced sentence. After serving his time, it appeared he had learned his lesson, as he had not been charged with, or suspected of taking part in, any crimes thereafter.

Piper leaned forward, turned on the radio, and adjusted the tuner until she found a song she liked, some 'head banging' hard rock track from decades ago. She rocked backward and checked her side-view mirror.

Lockhart turned off the radio.

She whipped her head toward the dashboard then eyeballed him. "We've been on the road for hours, and you haven't said a word. Can't I at least get some social interaction," she motioned, "through music?"

He continued his pursuit of memorizing everything he could about Bartlett.

"Besides, it's *my* truck we're riding in."

"Actually," his eyes skimmed the page, "it belongs to the county."

She shot him a look. "Seriously? You're going by the book on me?"

He read.

Piper sighed, sunk deeper into her seat, and alternated hands on the steering wheel, mumbling under her breath, "Getting fired back there is beginning to look a whole lot more appealing." In the next heartbeat, she snorted out a truncated laugh while covering her mouth.

Lockhart observed her.

She glanced his way. "That song brought back memories. That's all." Two moments passed. "Bristol, Jace, and me went out for a beer after work one night." She waved off her passenger. "Don't worry. We were off duty." She smiled while shaking her head. "Jace was a riot. It was open mic night, combined with karaoke, and he got up and sung," she pointed at the dashboard, "*that song.*"

Lockhart rotated his shoulders to see her more

squarely.

Piper chuckled. "He got up on stage and belted out that song like he was a rock star, hips gyrating and everything." Another snicker. "He stunk. He was off-key. He missed words, made up words, but just kept plodding ahead. There wasn't anyone in that bar who wasn't laughing. And he received a hearty round of applause as he walked off the stage." She glimpsed Lockhart. "Naturally, Bristol and I teased him, telling him the applause was because everyone was happy it was over with." Nodding, Piper turned somber as she focused on the cars ahead of her. "Good memories."

Lockhart stared through the windshield, thinking of his son. As reserved and professional as Jace was, when he decided it was time to have fun, the kid didn't hold back. Lockhart shot his driver a glance, turned on the radio—the same song was still playing—then went back to his work.

Piper spied the side of Lockhart's face, smiled, then turned back toward traffic. A tick later, she started strumming her fingers on the steering wheel, in tune with the melody.

• • •

Ninety Minutes Later...
Burleigh, Idaho
Burleigh, Idaho—a town of ten thousand—was

situated less than fifty miles from where Idaho met up with Nevada and Utah. In the past, the railroad and manufacturing had played a huge role in the town's prosperity. But now, food processing and banking comprised Burleigh's critical economic industries.

Piper stopped the Dodge at the curb, across the street from Roger E. Bartlett's mobile home. The dwelling was nothing special, but then again, none of the other mobile homes in this trailer park would have fetched any more money on the market. This northwestern part of Burleigh was the least affluent neighborhood in town. While residents had done a decent job of maintaining their property, there were still plenty of plastic toys, old bicycles, and other items littering the front yards and driveways. There was even a rusted washer and dryer setting on a front porch, looking as if they were part of the home's décor.

Bartlett's driveway was empty, and the shades were drawn on the single-story structure's windows. Ironically, the one known criminal on the block had the best-looking place—freshly painted white siding, newer black roof, clean, well-manicured front lawn, and no patches of dirt or brown spots from dogs either tearing up the grass or taking a leak.

Piper ran the Ram's column-mounted gearshift to 'Park' but kept the motor running. "Doesn't look like he's home."

Lockhart pivoted back and forth in his seat, cranking

his head left and right to take in the neighborhood.

She faced her boss. "Shouldn't we check in with local law enforcement? Let them know we're here."

"We're five days behind in solving Jace's murder. Every minute we wait," he shouldered his door open, "is another minute the trail to finding the killers goes cold." He got out, shut the door, and crossed in front of the Ram's grille, stopping at the vehicle's left-front corner.

Piper climbed down from the truck, put on her short, dark-brown fur-collared sheriff's jacket, and joined him. The skies were overcast here, and the temps were around fifty, but she zipped the coat against the stiff breeze driving a light rain. After hiking her gun belt higher up her waist, she glanced at Lockhart, "So, are we expecting trouble here?" before eyeballing the target's home.

"If he was involved in my son's death," Lockhart nodded once, "then expect trouble."

She spied her boss. "From *him*, or from *you*?"

Hearing her undertones, he glimpsed his undersheriff, then checked both ways, crossed the street, and headed up the driveway. "Keep your hand near your sidearm and your eyes on a swivel. I'm not losing another deputy."

For a moment, Piper's heart fluttered; however, if the circumstances hadn't been what they were, she would have fired off some good-humored comeback. Instead, she simply acknowledged him. "Roger that."

Lockhart noticed how small the stone steps were and

that there really was nowhere to stand that didn't place him in the 'fatal funnel' in line with the door. Without looking back, he gestured toward Piper. "Stay down here." He took the steps, tried to peek into windows, then pushed a doorbell before 'hugging' the black wrought iron railing to his right and rapping a knuckle on the locked screen door.

Down below, Piper had her open right hand on her Glock 19, looking as if she were simply standing with her hand on her hip. She kept pivoting her head, her eyes taking in everything she could while casting glances toward the home.

Once again, Lockhart rang the doorbell before banging on the door with his fist.

Ten seconds passed.

"I'll check around back." Piper went right and darted around the corner of the trailer.

Lockhart waited another 'five' then pounded on the door. He heard an engine behind him and turned.

A rattletrap red two-door truck, its tailgate missing, rumbled into the driveway.

Lockhart squinted at the driver, his mind envisioning the picture that had accompanied the rap sheet on Roger E. Bartlett—black stringy hair, gaunt features, and a dark goatee on a pointy chin. While the goatee was now absent, everything else matched.

Lockhart took the steps while poking his chin at the man. "Roger Bartlett?" Before he could get his next

        AMBUSH

sentence out, he saw the 'whites' of the man's eyes.

The man pivoted his upper body and navigated the truck back out of the driveway.

"Hey!" Lockhart drew his 44 Magnum Ruger Redhawk. "Sheriff's office. Stop right—"

The truck sped away, its tires spinning on the wet asphalt.

"Piper," shouted Lockhart, as he holstered his revolver and bolted for the Ram 1500 SSV.

Having heard the commotion, she had already cleared the home and was now running down the driveway, not ten feet behind Lockhart. She holstered her gun then pumped her arms as she picked up speed. Having taken part in track in high school, and still being an avid jogger, she showcased all the physical attributes of a world-class sprinter, catching up to him three feet from the truck, her eyes set on the driver's door.

"I'm driving." Lockhart threw open the door and jumped behind the wheel.

Piper veered left and rounded the Ram's front end, sticking two fingers into a slot on the grille to help slingshot her around the right-front corner. She hopped into the passenger seat, slammed her door, and affixed her seatbelt, her heart pounding, and her chest heaving.

He ran the gearshift to 'Drive' and smashed the gas pedal.

The Special Service Vehicle took off much the same way the other truck had, only this one did so with flashing lights and a blaring siren.

…

One Minute Later...

Lockhart and Piper had chased the red truck through three intersections, narrowly missing a crossing delivery van that had had a green light. The sheriff had to swerve right and go over a curb before bringing the Dodge Ram back onto the street.

Now he was making a sharp, hand-over-hand left turn onto a one-way street. Fortunately, they were going with the flow of traffic, but at this time of the day, traffic was picking up as schools were letting out and parents were travelling to pick them up.

Up ahead, the red truck weaved in and out of cars, slowing, then swerving around dawdling vehicles.

Some motorists honked horns; others made gestures.

Having the advantage of lights and a siren, except for one short-lived 'blockade,' Lockhart was able to knife his way through the sea of vehicles that were either stopping or moving to the side of the road. Seeing a straightaway, he poured on the gas and got right behind the fleeing truck.

Constantly whipping his head around to see his pursuer, Bartlett had a hard time keeping the truck from hitting other cars.

The red truck made a right onto a two-way street.

Lockhart followed.

And the two vehicles raced on.

Further down the road, seeing the fast-approaching trucks, a man hooked his female companion by the elbow and pulled her behind a parked car as the truck passed within a foot of hitting the couple.

Piper winced. "He's going to kill someone."

"Keep an eye out for cross traffic." Lockhart zoomed through another traffic light.

The red truck veered into oncoming traffic, zipped around a compact car, and returned to the right lane.

Lockhart spied several cars coming at him. Unable to make the same maneuver, he grimaced while hitting the brakes.

The compact ahead of the Dodge slowed but couldn't get over due to parked cars on its right.

He waited for oncoming traffic to pass or stop then accelerated around the tiny two-door, catching up to the red truck thirty seconds later.

Lockhart and Piper watched as the man alternated between shooting glances over his shoulder and searching for his next turnoff.

At the next crossroad, a four-way stop with tall buildings on all four corners, the getaway vehicle veered right then made a high-speed left-hand turn.

"He's not going to make it," said Lockhart. "He's going too fast."

The jalopy went into the turn on its right two wheels.

It sideswiped an SUV that had the right of way and had been entering the intersection from the truck's right. The collision both slowed and righted the tipping truck. It slammed back down onto all four tires, but still had enough momentum to skid sideways, jump a curb, and careen along the front of a brown brick building.

Grinding metal accompanied sparks as bystanders dove for cover.

Lockhart slowed, steering the Ram to the left, around the disabled SUV, then brought the 1500 SSV to a halt in the right lane, alongside a black Corvette, the stopped red truck on the opposite side of the sports car. He squinted at the mangled truck. "I don't see him."

Piper sent out her right pointer finger as she leaned left to see around the Dodge's door post on her one o'clock. "There he is."

Lockhart spotted a running Bartlett. "Got him." He hit the 'gas,' and the SSV took off again.

The fleeing man kept looking over his shoulder as he ran.

Seeing an opening among the parked cars, Lockhart pulled ahead, jerked the wheel to the right, and stepped on the brake pedal.

The 1500 screeched to an angled stop, its front end blocking the sidewalk, its rear tires still on the street.

Piper scrambled out, drew her Glock, and rushed to meet Bartlett head on.

Having had to put the vehicle into 'Park,' undo his

safety belt, and circle around the truck's front end, Lockhart was several paces behind his undersheriff.

Coming to a stutter stop and surveying his surroundings...

"Freeze!" Piper aimed her weapon at the man. "Sheriff's off—"

...Bartlett looked right then darted into a coffee house.

Piper followed, her gun at the low-ready position as she eased open the glass door, scanned the interior, then entered.

Seeing Piper go into the building, Lockhart glimpsed the name of the establishment, glanced behind him, then backed up to peek around the corner of the building. After a quick look at where Piper had gone, he took off running down a narrow alley between two structures.

•••

The coffee house was small, only big enough for a half a dozen round red bistro tables and twelve curved-back, round-seated red chairs in addition to the six, two-person booths that flanked the tables and chairs on the left and right sides of the space.

One booth was occupied by a couple, and three of the six bistro tables were taken up by a few people who had been chatting, pecking away at a laptop, or lost in whatever was on their cell phone.

Bartlett's storming of the coffee house had disturbed the casual conversations. He was now zigging and zagging his way around the tables while casting backward glances at the door.

Their drinks tipping over as the intruder rushed by them, some patrons cursed him out; others moved to get out of his way.

"Stop! Sheriff's Office." Piper wanted to raise her firearm, but there were people in her line of fire and directly beyond. She holstered the gun and darted forward, snaking around an overturned chair then sidestepping around a teetering table.

As he ran, Bartlett reached out and toppled chairs and tables behind him, spilling beverages and sending a silver laptop crashing to the floor.

Seeing her expensive property laying in a puddle of brown liquid, a young girl in her early twenties went off on a vulgarity-laden tirade at the man.

Bartlett dove onto the serving counter at the back of the establishment and slid off, falling to the floor on the other side.

The barista, another woman in her twenties with dark hair, tattoos, and piercings all over her face, retreated into a corner.

Piper leaped over a chair on its side, avoided the damaged laptop, then picked up speed. Like a gymnast performing a simple A-rated balance beam mount, she jumped, laid palms on the counter, and swung her legs up and to the left.

Bartlett had recovered and was now running along the counter toward the red 'EXIT' sign stationed at the back-right corner of the place.

Now squatting on all fours, Piper shot out of her stance and ran along the counter, dodging machines and knocking over cups and utensils while keeping one eye on her target on her eleven o'clock.

Bartlett made a rounded left-ninety, his right foot slipping a bit as he came out of his turn.

Piper hurdled an espresso machine, pushed off with her right foot, and extended her arms. Her boots landed with a thud two seconds later as she got a handful of Bartlett's unzipped gray hoodie.

With the left half of the hoodie being yanked from his body, the skinny five-nine, one-fifty man was knocked off balance, his right shoulder ramming into the wall on his three o'clock.

Having stumbled upon landing, but still grasping the hoodie in her left hand, Piper now threw out her free hand to steady herself on the wall.

Bartlett spun clockwise to free himself from his jacket.

Piper came at him.

He balled his half of the cotton clothing and shoved it toward her face.

Her head rocked backward as she bellowed out and raised her right hand to her nose.

Bartlett bolted away from her, drove his palms into the horizontal bar on the back door, and was gone.

Piper pulled her hand away from her nose and spied blood on her fingers. "Son-of-a—" she chased after him.

. . .

Outside, standing beside the coffee house's back door, opposite the door's hinged side, Lockhart heard a crash then saw the green metal door swing away from him as Bartlett fled the building.

Looking like a left-footed kicker attempting a 50-yard field goal, Lockhart tripped the man, his foot catching Bartlett's left shin.

Bartlett howled as he tumbled to the pavement. Rolling, he held his injured shin in both hands.

Lockhart pursued.

Piper exited two beats later, but pulled up when she noticed her boss.

Spotting red on her nose, lips, and chin, he met her gaze.

She waved him off. "I'm good. He just hit me in the nose."

Bartlett staggered to his feet and hobbled away.

Lockhart dogged him.

Bartlett tossed a couple backward glances while staggering away. Realizing his escape wasn't going to happen, he whirled around and threw out a roundhouse right.

Lockhart ducked under the wayward punch, got five fingers worth of a grubby, holey, black t-shirt and pulled while throwing a quick right jab to the man's mouth. "Punch my deputy, will you?" He reversed course and landed another jab, "And kill my son," before rearing back once more.

Piper grabbed his arm while spinning left to get between the men. Her back to Bartlett, "Stop," she said before tipping her head backward. "Over my right shoulder. You see her?"

He looked beyond her to see a woman holding up a cell phone in front of her face.

Piper pressed her right hand against Lockhart's chest. "Nosey Nancy over there wasn't quick enough to find the camera button to capture *all* the action, so you're still in the clear." A tick. "But let's do the rest of this by the book." She took hold of a wobbly Bartlett and handcuffed him. Searching his pockets, she took half-second breaks to wipe away the dripping blood from her nose.

Following another peek at the 'citizen journalist,' Lockhart nudged her out of the way while offering her his white handkerchief. "Take care of yourself. I'll search *him*."

She claimed the folded square, tipped her head back, and held the cloth to her bleeding nose. "Thanks."

AMBUSH

CHAPTER 6
My Request

Tom Schneider was a big man, both in height and width. Anyone foolish enough to tussle with him during an arrest usually found himself face down and bleeding from somewhere on his body.

At six-five, and tipping the scales at close to 250 pounds, the brown-haired, blue-eyed 50-year-old sheriff filled out the high-back chair behind his office desk. With the chair creaking and groaning in protest, he rocked forward, laid elbows on the desk, and covered his left fist with a meaty right hand. "I wish you would've come to me first. This is my county, and I'm the chief law enforcement officer around here."

With Piper occupying the straight-back leather chair on his nine o'clock, Lockhart gripped his chair's armrests. "I was in a hurry. We're already behind in this investigation. Surely, you can appreciate the importance of time in these matters."

Working his jaw back and forth, Schneider took a breath and nodded. "Yeah," a beat, "yeah, I suppose I can."

Lockhart tried to pull off a cordial smile. "Won't

happen again." He paused. "Now, how about my request?"

The local lawman tweaked his head once. "Bartlett's already lawyered up." He checked his watch. "I'm told his attorney will be here shortly." He confronted his male counterpart. "I can't let you talk to him without his lawyer present."

"Then I'll wait."

Schneider stared at Lockhart.

"I got nothing else to go on." Lockhart motioned behind him. "That guy's my only lead in finding the men who did this."

For the next ten seconds, both men leveled stoic gazes at each other.

Schneider finally glanced away while laying palms on his desk. He strummed his fingers then came back to his petitioner. "All right." He raised an index finger. "But only with his lawyer present. And when Bartlett says he's done, *you're* done."

Lockhart stood, "You got it," then made his way to the door, Piper on his heels.

"And Wade?"

Lockhart turned back.

"I'm sorry about your son."

Lockhart remained stone-faced.

"Jace and I crossed paths during a recent prisoner transfer. He was green, but," Schneider nodded, "he was extremely professional. He was on his way to becoming a top-rate deputy." Two pulses. "Anyway, I hope you catch those responsible."

Lockhart dipped his chin once and left the office.

● ● ●

Ten Minutes Later...

Lockhart and Piper walked down a carpeted hallway with white-painted walls and tubular lighting overhead. There was a single door at the far end of the 'runway.'

On her boss' right, Piper gave him a sideways glance. "I'm going in with you, Wade."

He shook his head. "That's not going to work."

"Neither is you reaching across the table and strangling our only lead."

He pulled up and faced her. "Look, I get what you're doing. I know you're only trying to protect me," he twisted his neck once, "mostly from myself."

She crossed her arms. "And you're not making it any easier."

"But your presence," he pointed at the door, "in there is only going to be an unnecessary distraction for Bartlett. I have a plan, a few pressure points I can leverage. But for that tack to work, I need for him to feel alone—*on an island*—and that I'm his only chance at survival."

Piper bit her lower lip and groaned. Moments later, "Fine," she aimed a finger at his nose. "But I'll be watching, ready to barge in if I need to."

Lockhart huffed. "Oh, I," grabbing the doorknob, he looked back at her, "I *know* you will." He opened the door and entered the room.

•••

Void of anything but a metal table and four metal folding chairs, with dim overhead lighting and a wide mirror on the wall, the 12-by-12 room had a sterile, cold feel to it, perfect for making sure detainees didn't get too comfortable.

Lockhart closed the door behind him, the act reverberating off hard surfaces. Standing tall, he studied the others in the room.

Roger Bartlett sat facing the mirror, handcuffed to the table, while his attorney, a late-twenties woman wearing an off-the-rack navy-blue skirt suit, heels to match, and a white blouse, sat on his right. She had short blonde hair, a round, freckled face, and 'squinty' eyes thick with eye liner and mascara. A closed black briefcase sat on the floor beside her crossed legs covered with flesh-colored pantyhose.

Lockhart studied her hazel eyes, eyes he was sure were attractive in the daylight. But here, in this gloomy setting, they betrayed a newly minted public defender who was eager to advance her career, eager to portray vast legal experience he was confident she did not yet possess.

The sheriff pulled out a chair from under the table and sat directly across from Bartlett. Following a brief nonverbal back-and-forth with the lawyer, he laid forearms on the table and interlaced his fingers.

"I don't know what you hope to accomplish here, Sheriff, but my client has nothing to say to you."

A defiant Bartlett sat back in his seat, his arms folded across his chest, a sneer on his face.

"That's fine." Lockhart zeroed in on his prey. "I'll do the talking."

The lawyer struck a similar pose as Bartlett then lowered her head.

Lockhart cocked his head to the left. "We have dashcam footage clearly showing you seated in the backseat of that sedan. The FBI has all but confirmed you were present when my s—when my *deputy* was murdered." He poked a finger at Bartlett. "At the very least, that makes you an accessory to killing a law enforcement official, a serious crime."

The lawyer leaned toward her client. "Say nothing. I have yet to review this footage. It could be grainy and out-of-focus or just plain wrong."

Lockhart eyeballed the woman before coming back to Bartlett. "Your attorney is giving you bad legal advice, Roger." He let a few moments pass. "On the other hand, I'm here to give you an alternative. Don't misunderstand me. You *are* going to prison. There's no way around that.

It's out of our hands." More time passed. "But the length of your sentence, and where you serve out that sentence, *is* in our control—*your* control, in fact." Lockhart saw Bartlett tip his head to the side ever so slightly. *Good. I have your attention now.*

"You see," continued Lockhart, "I know you didn't pull the trigger that night. And I want the trigger man. But," he held a shrug while turning his palms toward the ceiling, "if you don't help me find him, then I'm going to push for you to be charged as if you were solely responsible for the murder of my deputy."

Bartlett swallowed, glanced at his attorney, then returned to the sheriff.

"So, here's my offer. Tell me what happened that night, give me the names of the men who were with you, and where I can find them, and I'll go to bat for you with the prosecuting attorney. I'll recommend a reduced sentence in a not-so-hardened facility."

Bartlett met his lawyer's gaze.

She wrinkled her nose and shook her head. "He's trying to coerce you into incriminating yourself. Trust me. After I've had a chance to review all the evidence against you, we'll have options."

"Not true," said Lockhart. "The only option you have is my offer. And that's only available for as long as I'm in this room. And I'm not bluffing." He squinted at Bartlett. "With or without your assistance, I *will* find the others, Roger. But that won't matter to you, though, because your fate will have already been sealed. I'll make sure *all of you* get the death penalty."

"*Death* penalty?" said Bartlett.

Lockhart noted a couple of sweat beads forming on the man's forehead. "Yep. Deliberate homicide committed against a peace officer killed in the line of duty is punishable by death."

"Whoa, whoa, whoa. Hold on now." As much as he could, Bartlett raised his hands in surrender, his chains rattling. "I never killed that cop. I swear."

"Stop talking," chided the woman before facing Lockhart. "We're done here. My client has nothing further to say."

Bartlett leaned forward in his chair. "Will you really go to bat for me?"

"Help me, and I'll help you," replied Lockhart.

"Don't say anything else," said the woman to her client.

Bartlett tipped his head to one side. "How do I know I can trust you?"

Lockhart shrugged. "You don't. All I can give you is my word."

Bartlett thought.

"This interview is over, Sheriff," said the lawyer. "You have no authority to keep badgering my client like this. This is unaccept—"

"Shut up," said Bartlett. "This is *my* life on the line here. *I'll* decide when this interview is over." He eyed the lawman across from him.

Lockhart looked him square in the eye. "If you cooperate here and now, you have my word I'll do what I can for you," a tick, "as much as you have my word that I'll use every means at my disposal to make sure you *fry* for killing my deputy if you *don't* cooperate." He arched his brows. "And I'm *definitely* a man of my word?"

Roger Bartlett sat hunched over, holding his head in his hands. He rocked back and forth in his chair for the next several seconds. The chains securing his handcuffs to the bolt anchored to the metal table jangled in the quiet interrogation room.

Lockhart slid his chair backward. The furniture's rubber-padded legs half slid, and half skidded, over the dirty tile floor, filling the room with a hair-raising, squawking eruption that bounced off the walls.

Bartlett raised his head to see the lawman turning toward the door. "Where are you going?"

Lockhart strolled toward the door.

"I said, *where* are you going?" The restrained man recalled the sheriff's words...*only available for as long as I'm in this room. And I'm not bluffing.* "All right, all right. I'll talk."

Lockhart stopped. "No games, Roger. I want it all."

"I promise. I'll tell you everything I know. Just don't leave."

Lockhart came back to the table, took his seat, and retrieved a small notebook and pen from his jacket pocket. He flipped to the start of clean pages, clicked the pen, and sat poised to write as he regarded Bartlett. "Let's begin by you giving me the names of those who were in the vehicle with you when my deputy was killed."

Bartlett shook his head. "I don't know the name of the driver, the one who did the shooting. In fact, I had never met him before. But Nick kept calling him Sledge."

"Who's Nick?"

"He was the guy in the passenger seat."

"What's Nick's last name?"

"Castellano. He's originally from Philadelphia, I think. I've worked with him on other jobs. He called to tell me about this job that was supposed to go down in Montana."

"Where can I find this Nick?" asked Lockhart, his pen scrawling across the pages of his notepad as he wrote.

Bartlett scrunched up his brow. "I don't know where he lives. But I do know he has a girlfriend in Roseburg."

"Idaho?" prompted Lockhart.

"Uh-huh." A beat. "I'm not sure how much they're in a real relationship as much as they're in a," he faltered, "a sexual arrangement, you could say."

Lockhart raised his brows.

"She's a dancer and a hooker. And based on how he talks about her, I'm thinking she falls into the hooker category with him."

"What's the dancer-slash-hooker's name?"

"Missy something. I never heard a last name."

"You said she dances," Lockhart flipped over a page, "in Roseburg?"

Bartlett nodded.

"Where does she dance?"

The handcuffed man glanced away for a couple of seconds before facing the sheriff. "Queens Over Aces. I think it's on the eastern side of the city."

Lockhart pivoted right in his chair to glance at the mirror, his mind envisioning Piper watching him. "Nick Castellano, Sledge, Missy," he rolled an index finger, "find out everything you can," before turning back around while going back a couple pages. "You said there was some job that was supposed to go down in Montana. What job?"

"Nick called me and told me there was easy money up in Montana. Some old guy with a huge stash of guns was going to be out of town. I was to steal a car and drive while Nick and this Sledge dude broke in and stole the guns. Nick told me he already had a buyer for the guns. It was supposed to be a three-way split."

"What's the address of the home where you stole the guns?"

Bartlett shrugged. "I wasn't told."

"Then how'd you drive there?" asked Lockhart.

"That's just it. We *didn't*. After that cop stopped us, the whole operation was," he cursed. "We just ended up driving to where I had previously staged a stolen car; the one we were supposed to use after the robbery. Nick took some gas cans out of the trunk, doused the vehicle," he pointed at Lockhart, "the one we were riding in when that Sledge guy shot that cop. Then he lit it on fire. I was given some money and told to keep my mouth shut and that if anyone finds out, I'd be just as guilty as the others." He shrugged. "After that, we all went our separate ways." Bartlett stared at Lockhart. "Like I told you, Sheriff. I'm no killer. I never killed that cop." A pulse. "So, are you going to go to bat for me...like you said you would?"

"I have a few more questions," a tick, "and I still need to verify your story." Lockhart scratched his chin then wrote on his notepad. "But if everything checks out, then," he confronted Bartlett, "yes, I'll do everything I can."

•••

One Hour Later...

Having been granted temporary login credentials to local law enforcement's terminal access, Piper had worked to uncover Nick Castellano's last known address; however, upon contacting the apartment manager, she had been informed that Nick had moved out a month ago and had not left a forwarding address. Piper had then asked Sheriff Schneider to issue a statewide 'BOLO' for Nick Castellano.

Moving on to the stripper/hooker named Missy, Piper had contacted the woman's place of employment, Queens Over Aces, and discreetly asked about a dancer named Missy. Portraying someone who was specifically requesting Missy for a guy's bachelor party, Piper had been able to confirm there was indeed a Missy who danced there.

Going further, Piper had then contacted the Roseburg Police Department, asking about any sex workers by the name of Missy operating out of Roseburg. As it turned out, Missy was the middle name of a prostitute named Kristina Walters who lived in the northeast part of Roseburg, Idaho, close to her job at the strip club.

Finally, with only 'Sledge' to go on, Piper had done her best to locate any criminals with that street name in Idaho and the nearby states of Wyoming and Montana; however, her efforts had been in vain.

Now, standing in Sheriff Schneider's office, Lockhart shook the man's hand. "Much obliged for the assistance, Tom."

Schneider pumped his counterpart's hand twice and let go. "Glad I could help. And good luck on your investigation."

Donning his cowboy hat, "Speaking of that," Lockhart tugged on the brim, "if you hear anything, I'd appreciate a call."

Schneider bobbed his head once. "Safe travels."

Lockhart acknowledged him and left the office.

"Thank you for the use of your computer system," said Piper.

"My pleasure, Ma'am."

•••

Outside, an hour away from sunset, the temps had dropped a couple degrees, and the light rain had picked up, as Lockhart and Piper hurried toward her Dodge Ram parked on the street near the sheriff's office.

Lockhart noticed an oncoming car cruising close to the sidewalk. He caught Piper by the arm and pulled her away from a nearby puddle.

The car's right tires hit the puddle and sent a water spray into the air, the arch narrowly missing the out-of-town LEOs.

"Well, that would've sucked," said Piper.

He gave each way another glance before heading across the street. "You drive."

Once behind the wheel, Piper affixed her seat belt, fired up the truck, then hovered over the dashboard computer keyboard. "Where to first...where she lives or strips?"

Lockhart settled into his seat. "When you called the club, did the manager say if this *Missy* was working tonight?"

"I never asked. Didn't want to risk spooking her if he ended up talking to her."

He nodded then checked his watch. "Roseburg's two hours away." A tick. "By the time we roll into town, the night scene should be heating up."

Piper entered the address for Queens Over Aces into the truck's onboard navigation system, "Strip club it is then," before turning on the windshield wipers and pulling away from the curb, the Ram's wipers clearing away a steady wash of water from the glass.

Two hours north of Burleigh, the forty thousand residents of Roseburg were stuck in a stormy weather pattern. Temperatures were hovering around the freezing mark, and the falling rain was doing its best to turn into a wintry, slushy mix. Fortunately for Lockhart and Piper, they were now standing under a covered walkway. Raising a hand, he rapped a cheap, brass-colored door knocker against a white metal door.

Seconds later, the door opened, and a woman's head peeked out from around the door's edge. With her long black curly hair hanging down over her left shoulder, and stopping at her left elbow, the woman wore heavy makeup—eye shadow, eyeliner, mascara, cheek blush, thick red lipstick—the works. "Who are *you*?" she snapped.

Having gone to Queens Over Aces and spoken to the strip club's manager, who had informed them that Kristina Walters was not scheduled to work for the next two days, Lockhart and Piper had then driven to the woman's apartment.

On Piper's nine o'clock, Lockhart pulled back the

right half of his leather jacket to reveal the Big Sky County sheriff's badge affixed to his belt, just forward of his Ruger Redhawk revolver. "Sheriff Lockhart, Ma'am." He motioned toward Piper. "This is my undersheriff, Ms. Jennings." He jabbed his chin at the woman's head. "Are you Kristina Walters?"

"Yeah. What's this about?"

"We'd like to ask you a few questions."

"About what?"

"Nick Castellano."

Her eyes got bigger. "Have you seen him?"

"We were hoping *you* could tell us how to find him."

"I wish I knew. He owes me for this month's rent, and my landlord is up my," she cursed, "about it."

"May we discuss this inside?"

Kristina gave Piper a long look before coming back to Lockhart. A tick later, she held out her left hand. "Your badge," a pulse, "let me see it."

He shot Piper a sideways look then faced the other woman. "Ma'am?"

"Do you want to come in or not?"

Two seconds passed.

Lockhart unclipped his badge and forfeited it.

Kristina examined his credentials like a jeweler trying to spot a fake diamond. She then held the badge in her palm and pumped her hand up and down a few times before returning Lockhart's property to him. "All right. Seems legit." She spun around while opening the door wider. "Come on in."

Piper's brows rose higher at the sight of what Kristina was wearing.

Lockhart stepped into the small apartment, one of several all lined up in a row and parallel with the street. A small parking lot sat between the apartment building and the street. Two rusting lamp posts, twenty feet away from each other, were anchored to the concrete in the center of the lot. Neither one did a very good job at lighting up the area. He was sure if he dug into the building's ownership records, he would discover the structure had once been a motel.

"So, why do you want Nicky?" asked Kristina, her back to her guests. Standing in front of a brown, tattered cloth sofa, she bent over, sunk her left heel into a cushion, then pulled a black stocking over her painted toes before sliding the sheer fabric up her left calf.

"One of my deputies was murdered," replied Lockhart, "and we believe Mr. Castellano may have information that might help us find out who did it."

Closing the door behind her, Piper gave the tenant another wild-eyed glance then shot a look at Lockhart. To her surprise, he was unfazed by the 'skin show.' In fact, he was slowly taking in the tiny apartment's amenities, something she should have been doing too if she hadn't been thrown off her game at how the woman had answered the doorbell—wearing only a black thong.

"Don't mind me." Kristina donned a second stocking.

"My ride's going to be here any minute, and I need to get ready." A pulse. "So, a cop got killed, huh? That sucks."

Sucks indeed, thought Lockhart while noting simple furnishings—couch, easy chair, side table, television, and a few pictures on the light-colored walls. None of the pictures matched, and all were haphazardly placed. If he had to guess, they had been hung to cover holes in the walls. He did take note of several items in the room that clearly belonged to a man—shoes, clothing, and a few other things that appeared to have more monetary value. "When was the last time you saw Nick Castellano, Ms. Walters?"

Kristina stepped into a black miniskirt and wriggled the tight-fitting garment up her legs and over her hips, hips that were quite wide for the petite, five-foot-nothing, slender woman that she was. Bare-chested, she faced her questioner while zipping the skirt.

Getting a side view of smallish, pointy breasts, Piper rubbed her forehead while watching Lockhart from behind her palm. She followed his line-of-sight straight to the half-naked woman's eyes. *Dang. He's got more restraint than I do. And I'm not into chicks.*

Kristina closed one eye and looked toward the ceiling. "Three," she hesitated, "no, four days ago, I think. He spent the night here and left in the morning. Haven't seen him since."

"Is that normal for him?"

"He's usually here every night." A moment. "Actually,

I'm starting to think the little," she uttered a vulgar euphemism, "bailed on me."

"Are you two in a relationship?" asked Piper.

Kristina scooped up a black, strapless midriff corset and placed it against her bosom. "Not in the traditional sense. He started coming around Queens, requesting lap dances from me." With her right hand, she lifted her left breast and let it plop into the corset's corresponding molded cup before moving on to her right one. "During the dances I gave him, we got to talking. He said he needed a place to live and that he could pay." She shrugged. "I needed the extra money, and he seemed harmless, so I let him move in here." She gave Lockhart a slow down-and-up. "Hey, big fella," she pivoted clockwise while cranking her head to her left and giving him a sultry smile over her shoulder, "how about zipping me up?"

A curious Piper observed her boss.

He dialed up a slow, methodical shake of his head. "Not a chance, Ms. Walters."

She faked a pout before reaching around behind her and finagling the zipper up to where she could finish the task with arms over her shoulders.

"Are you and Mr. Castellano," Lockhart paused, "intimate?"

Kristina grabbed a couple of dark-red, five-inch-high, spiked pumps and turned out her left leg to wiggle her left foot into the footwear. "Like I told," she jerked her head toward Piper, "*her*, over there, not in the traditional sense." After throwing out her right leg and twisting her right shoe onto her foot, she stood tall, slid arms into a short, dark-red leather jacket, flipped out her long hair, and adjusted the coat's lapels. She squinted at the lawman. "Are you here to bust me for hooking?"

Lockhart shook his head. "No, Ma'am. Just looking for Nick Castellano."

She took a few seconds to study him and Piper before she picked up a small red clutch purse and began dropping personal care items into the bag. "When Nicky wants to, he and I *hook up*, if you know what I mean. He pays for it, of course. I don't give out freebies."

Piper bobbed her eyebrows and said, her tone dripping with sarcasm, "Always good to have multiple streams of income."

Kristina stabbed a finger at Piper. "Don't you *dare* judge me, you," she cursed. "Unless you want to pay my rent and put food on the table, then just shut the," another curse, "up. We all don't get to play," she waved a hand at Piper while snarling at her clothing, "cop lady. Some of us haven't had the best breaks in life. Some of us have had to—"

"Ms. Walters," interjected Lockhart.

The woman whipped her head toward him, her scowl fading a moment later.

"Do you have a way to reach Mr. Castellano?"

"Never asked for one." She picked up a tube of

lipstick and pitched it into her purse. "The only communicating we do is between the sheets or when the rent is due."

Lockhart laid hands on his hips and inventoried the apartment once more, his eyes settling on a framed picture near the sofa. "Well, Ms. Walters, thank you for your time. We'll let you finish getting ready." He caught Piper's attention then swung a finger from her to Kristina. "Please call us if you happen to see Mr. Castellano."

Piper dug out a business card from her jacket and held it out to Kristina.

Glaring at Piper, the dolled-up woman snatched the card from her female counterpart's fingers. "Sure thing."

"Once again," said Lockhart while opening the apartment door, "thank you for your time."

Lockhart and Piper exited the apartment and climbed into her Dodge Ram.

"She didn't *look* or *act* like she was covering for Castellano," said Piper. "As long as he pays his rent, she—" Piper huffed, "and leaves a twenty on the nightstand while she's showering, she couldn't care less about him."

"*He* doesn't think that way about *her*."

Piper frowned at him. "What are you talking about? He's sleeping on her couch." She tipped her head from side to side. "And paying her for sex."

Lockhart observed his undersheriff while pointing

toward Kristina's apartment. "There was an expensive men's gold watch on the table in there. Had to be worth several hundred dollars, if not more."

Piper held a shrug. "So?"

"So, my guess is it belongs to Castellano, and that's his way of showing he trusts her."

"She could've lifted that off one of her Johns."

"If that were true," he replied, "then she would've already hawked it for money." A beat. "Plus, there was a framed photo of her and Castellano in an embrace."

Having noticed the photo as well, Piper scoffed. "Wade, she was naked from the waist up in that photo. Guys get those taken at the clubs so they can brag to their buddies. They're trophy shots."

"And do most guys put those *trophy shots* in frames with little red hearts on them?"

She hunched her shoulders. "Maybe he found that somewhere in the apartment. I don't know."

Looking out his window, Lockhart laid his right elbow on the door and washed a hand down his face, his mind recalling how often he had thought about Jace since his son's murder. Sometimes, it felt as if his boy was still alive, off patrolling the roads of Big Sky County. Lockhart had even dialed Jace's cell phone on two occasions, only to come to his senses halfway through and thumb the 'End' button. "Sometimes," he scratched his chin while gawking at the darkness outside, "men see things as they want them to be," a beat, "not as they *are*."

Noting his distant, brooding tone, Piper half wondered if he was still talking about their suspect. She blinked twice and shook her head. "Well, if Castellano thinks she's in love with him, then he's in for a hard fall." Piper eyed Kristina's apartment. "What do we do now?"

Lockhart turned away from his window to stare at what his employee was eyeballing. "Now we stay put and watch Ms. Walters."

Piper faced him. "A stakeout?"

He nodded. "If my theory on Castellano is right, then sooner or later, he'll be making contact with her."

"And if he doesn't?"

"He will."

"Okay," Piper pumped open hands downward, "for the sake of argument, let's say you're right. It could be days before he shows up."

Lockhart got comfortable. "You chose a career in law enforcement." A beat. "Welcome to law enforcement."

She let out a long sigh.

"Find somewhere to park this thing, so we're out of sight when he shows."

Piper started the truck and drove out of her parking spot. "*If* he shows."

Lockhart reclined his seat then brought his hat down over his eyes. "*When* he shows."

FOUR HOURS LATER

Four hours ago, Lockhart and Piper had watched Kristina Walters leave her apartment and climb into the backseat of an expensive four-door luxury sedan. He chose not to follow, because wherever she was going, she wasn't going to see Nick Castellano, dressed to the nines.

The stakeout had been a quiet one, with each person taking turns getting some rest while the other watched the apartment. When Kristina had returned an hour ago, in the same sedan that had picked her up four hours earlier, both Lockhart and Piper had stayed awake. Each squirmed to get more comfortable in between taking sips of coffee that she had slipped out and purchased. Neither one had been hungry.

The atmosphere inside the Ram was somewhere between a funeral and that feeling you get when you're about to meet the parents of your boyfriend or girlfriend for the first time.

In the driver's seat, Piper rolled onto her left butt cheek. Five seconds later, she rolled back and took a drink of coffee.

Recalling the day's events, Lockhart shifted his gaze

to peep at her out of his left eye. He faced forward, cleared his throat, then filled his lungs, exhaling a moment later.

She sipped coffee then returned her beverage to its cup holder.

After giving her another glance, he covered his mouth with his right hand, then stroked his chin before intertwining forearms across his chest. "Listen, I uh," he swallowed, "about what I said earlier today," a beat, "back at the office," another beat, "my behavior toward you was—"

"Asinine?"

He confronted her.

She threw up her hands, "Sorry," then gestured toward him. "Continue."

He looked down at his Ariats. "I was going to say *unprofessional*, but," his eyebrows bounced once, "your take on the matter is spot-on as well."

"Everyone knows you're not yourself, Wade. You've been through hell."

He regarded his undersheriff; a woman he knew he was going to hire five minutes into her first and only interview. *'I have a few other interviews that I've promised people, but don't accept any other jobs,'* he had said to her at the end of the meeting.

"Piper, you're an intelligent and hard-working person. I knew that within minutes of first meeting you six years ago, when I hired you."

Piper glanced down at her fingernails as she drew her lips into her mouth to keep her heart from exploding out of her chest.

"And you get along with everyone in the office." His arms still crossed, he reached up and dragged a thumb over his chin. "You'd make an excellent sheriff." A beat. "Who knows? One day, we might end up campaigning *against* each other."

She whipped off a single, forceful headshake. "Never. If I ever do run for sheriff, it'll be *after* you've decided to leave office. I'd *never* betray you like that."

Lockhart nodded at her, the left corner of his mouth ticking higher. *Add loyalty to your long list of attributes.* Two pulses. "So, I apologize; however, until I can resolve," he faltered, "what's going on," a moment, "I'm afraid I can't promise I won't go off on you again."

Piper leaned sideways and touched his arm. "I know. Just take care of yourself. And if I can do anything to help," she squeezed his arm, "please ask."

He nodded, "Thank—" before squinting out his window, toward his two o'clock, into the slushy sleet that was collecting on everything that hadn't retained enough daytime heat to burn it off.

She lifted her gaze to see what had grabbed his attention. A second later, quickly pecking away at the Ram's computer terminal, she brought up a picture and went back and forth from the image to a man approaching the apartment complex from across the street. "That's him. That's Castellano." She dimmed the screen. "How do we play this?"

With the Ram 1500 SSV parked at the back of the lot, in the shadows, Lockhart spied Kristina Walters' apartment door on his eleven o'clock. She hadn't left since being dropped off. He glimpsed a fast-walking Castellano on his one o'clock, the man's path taking him straight for the woman's dwelling. "We intercept him." Lockhart shouldered open his door. "We don't want a hostage situation."

· · ·

Moments Later...
Piper had gone wide left and was just now bypassing the long row of apartments, Kristina Walters' corner place at the far end of the covered walkway.

After easing his door shut, Lockhart had gone straight across the parking lot, five vehicles on his left and two parked near the street on his right. His strides long, his head tipped slightly downward, he watched Castellano from under the brim of his Resistol hat while flexing and relaxing his fingers as he walked.

Coming up on Lockhart's twelve o'clock, the man turned his head to the left to give the man in the black leather jacket and blue jeans a casual glance. Three steps later, his attention turned toward the apartment, toward a woman wearing a brown fur-collared coat, her gun belt clearly visible in the outdoor overhead lighting.

Lockhart picked up his pace while veering left to slip between two parked cars.

Castellano slowed, his head rotating left then right, before he stopped.

Noticing Piper draw up to Kristina's door, Lockhart emerged from between the cars and continued his advance, bypassing the bumpers of two more vehicles.

Castellano backpedaled.

"Nick Castellano," barked Lockhart. "Sheriff's Office."

The tall and lanky Castellano turned and ran back the way he had come.

Lockhart bolted after him.

Piper sprinted away from the apartments, her arms pumping.

Thirty seconds later, the chase had taken Lockhart to the next street over. With Piper having almost caught up with him, he rounded the corner of a brick building on his right and spotted his prey. "Stop right there. Sheriff's office."

Still running away, the fleeing man spun right and threw out his right arm.

Breathing hard, Piper drew up on Lockhart's left, her momentum carrying her past him.

He clutched her jacket and pulled her behind the building.

Several gunshots rang out, a few shattering the

windshield of a parked truck directly behind where Piper had been moments ago.

Lockhart and Piper drew their weapons.

He peeked around the corner of the building to see Castellano getting behind the wheel of a sleek, low-to-the-ground Mazda MX-5 Miata. Lockhart raced forward to stretch out his arms across the hood of a Chevy Malibu, his revolver in both hands.

The Mazda backed up.

He fired three 44 Magnums at the vehicle's front grille.

The car turned right, toward Lockhart's eleven o'clock, and took off.

Lockhart fired twice more, the second 240-grain hollow soft point bullet penetrating the race car's left-front tire. He cocked the Redhawk's hammer, squeezed the double-action revolver's Hogue Monogrip tighter, and closed his right eye. A half second later, he eased off a shot.

The gun bucked and roared, a brilliant fireball spewing from the Ruger's 4.2-inch stainless-steel barrel.

The left-rear tire on the Miata blew out as the car sped away, the machine jerking left and right while lurching forward and backward.

"Go get the truck." Lockhart swung open the Redhawk's cylinder while turning the muzzle skyward. Using his right palm, he gave the ejector a firm slap—six empty cases fell to the pavement—before he retrieved a black plastic speedloader from his jacket pocket. Walking away from the Chevy, while lining up the noses of the six bullets with the weapon's six chambers, he pushed until all six cartridges released from the speedloader and fell into place.

"Where are you going?" said Piper.

Closing the cylinder, he returned the empty speedloader to his jacket pocket, then holstered his gun, "wherever *he's* going," before tearing after the escaping MX-5.

...

Minutes Later...

Lockhart came upon the Mazda parked sideways, its rear end blocking the street, its front end having crashed into a red minivan, steam billowing out from under the car's hood, the minivan's horn honking out a rhythmic tune. From one street over, he had heard the crash and followed the noise of the alarm.

From a nearby building, a man in shorts and a t-shirt stepped out onto the street. "Are you okay?"

Standing at the Mazda's open driver's door, Lockhart glanced down at barely visible footsteps in the quickly gathering slush. "Sheriff's office." He left the vehicle and followed the footprints onto the sidewalk.

After revealing his badge to the man, "Go back inside and dial nine-one-one," the lawman trailed the tracks a half a block down the street to where they stopped at a six-foot-high, chain-link fence that surrounded a construction site. He hauled out his cell phone and dialed Piper.

"Where are you?" she said.

"Follow that car alarm you hear."

"Hold on a second."

He heard what sounded like wind blowing through an open window.

"Okay, I hear it," she said.

"I trailed Castellano to a construction site. Contact me when you get here." He pinched his phone shut, stowed it in a jacket pocket, then climbed the fence. After rolling over the horizontal bar, while throwing out his legs, he landed on the other side of the fence, his eyes scanning, his ears listening.

There were several concrete pillars, three feet square and rising several stories into the air, each a support column for whatever kind of building that would eventually be erected here. Up above, two more floors had been started but were incomplete. Wheelbarrows, shovels, rakes, all sorts of tools and supplies were resting against unfinished interior concrete walls or laying stacked up under blue tarps, the tarps' corners flapping in the wind.

Lockhart drew his Ruger. *It's like a mini maze.* He advanced along the right side of the columns. At each one, he stopped and listened before moving on to the next.

The wind swirled around the columns and walls. Rain-snow pellets pinged off plastic tarps and metal wheelbarrows. Ambient light from the surrounding streetlights cast shadows in some places while exposing what lie in other areas.

Lockhart hurried toward the last column ahead of him, his boots either slapping at puddles or sloshing through a watery sludge.

Gunshots pierced the sounds of nature.

Bullets skipped off the pavement ahead of him.

Instinctively, he pulled up then raced forward to put his back to the last three-foot-wide column. "Drop your weapon and come out with your hands up, Castellano," a beat, "before this gets any worse."

More gunshots, one taking a chip out of the corner of the column.

Lockhart spun right while ducking lower. He fired three rounds at where he had seen muzzle flashes out of the corner of his eye—when he was running for shelter—before he spun back to safety.

Bullets ricocheted off the column near his right knee.

He returned a volley then opened his Ruger's cylinder, repeating the reloading process and then closing the cylinder. His back to concrete, he pivoted left to see another column kitty corner from him. It was further to his right and closer to Castellano. More columns were lined up on Lockhart's eleven o'clock, trailing away from him. But beyond that first one, on his two o'clock, there was open space leading to the back half of the construction site where there was another chain-link fence.

A single incoming round skittered off the pavement to Lockhart's right.

Designed to get him to expose himself, Lockhart didn't fall for the trick. He snaked around the corner to his left, drew up to the next corner, and fired two shots before bolting for the support structure on his two o'clock.

• • •

Piper clambered up and over the fence before landing on her boots and drawing her Glock 19. She had heard the gunshots before she had even put the Dodge Ram into 'Park.'

Now, she took in her surroundings.

A single gunshot came from her ten o'clock, followed by two louder booms from her twelve o'clock. She faced her twelve o'clock, *Wade*, then darted for the first concrete column, whipped out her cell phone, and dialed Lockhart's number.

• • •

Feeling a vibration coming from his jacket pocket,

Lockhart took out his phone and thumbed it open. "Where are you?" he said, his voice low.

"I just scaled the fence, and I'm behind some pillar. Going off the reports I'm hearing, I think I have a fix on both you and Castellano."

"Good. When I start firing, you head left and come up on his right flank. I'm circling in from his left."

"Copy that," replied Piper.

Lockhart closed his phone and stuffed it into his coat. He then opened the Redhawk's cylinder. Holding the weapon parallel with the pavement, but with its muzzle tipped slightly downward, he thumbed the ejector an inch then let go.

The heavier cartridges slid back into their chambers while the lighter, empty cases were left protruding from the cylinder. Pulling them from the wheel gun, he dropped them, then reached into his open jacket to pluck two individual cartridges from the loops securing the ammo to the brown leather ammo slide riding on his belt at the five o'clock position.

After topping off his revolver, Lockhart once again inched his way around one corner of the column then peeked around the next corner. He raised his revolver and emptied the gun in a slow, even rate of fire, his mind envisioning Piper running from column to column.

Having now spent the two speedloaders from his jacket pocket, Lockhart lifted the flap on a circular leather pouch riding on his belt at the four o'clock position, just behind his holster. He retrieved another speedloader and reloaded his gun.

• • •

Running all out, Piper pulled up short at the last support column. At the last second, her left boot hit a slick patch, and she skidded past her cover. After nearly doing the splits, she fell into a puddle before rolling into a mound of slush. *Damn it.* Looking up, she saw Castellano staring back at her.

The man stretched out his right arm toward her.

Flashes of light accompanied the cracks of several nine-millimeter rounds.

Flat on her stomach, the column three feet away on her right, Piper spotted an overturned wheelbarrow six feet away on her eleven o'clock.

Incoming rounds skipped off the pavement, sending puffs of sloppy mush into the air.

She barrel-rolled left, to get the wheelbarrow between her and Castellano, then army crawled through a battlefield of wet, sloppy terrain, her jeans soaking up water like a cotton towel. Now, with her back to the wheelbarrow's bed, she pivoted left and stuck her Glock out between the pushcart's two handles jutting out at different angles. Piper fired five rounds then retreated to glimpse the thin metal between her and Castellano. *His nines will punch right through this.* "Wade," she shouted.

"I'm pinned down and taking fire! Whatever you got planned..."

...

Piper's voice: "...do it now!"

Lockhart had a plan, but the fear in his undersheriff's voice compelled him to toss that plan and just plain act. He bolted from cover, bypassed the next column, then skidded to a halt halfway between the last two columns. Darting left, he stopped ten paces later to stand in the open, among the columns, his gun aimed at the backside of his suspect. "Castellano," he bellowed. "Drop the gun."

Castellano whirled around and got off a snapshot.

Lockhart worked his Ruger's trigger twice, and two 44 Magnums slammed into Castellano.

The man fell back against a column, clutching his chest, before dropping to his knees and landing face first in a puddle of water and slush.

Approaching Castellano, Lockhart kicked the man's gun away, then hurried around the support pillar. "Piper, we're clear." A tick. "Piper?"

...

Lockhart's voice: "Talk to me, Piper. Are you—"

"I'm," rolling to her knees, "ok—" Piper put her hand down to stand, "ow!" Something bit her palm, and she

ALEX ANDER

retracted her hand. "I'm okay." Examining her sore spot, but not seeing any blood, she stood and glanced down the length of her body.

Her jeans were drenched, and her jacket was covered in a mixture of dirt, water, and wet snow. She holstered her firearm then flapped her arms.

Moments later, she met up with Lockhart before glancing down at Castellano. "I take it he's..."

Lockhart nodded. "And we're left without our next lead in finding the man who killed Jace."

The door opened and Kristina Walters stood wearing a fluffy, powder-blue bathrobe that went from her neck to her ankles. Her black hair was wet and straight, the ends beginning to twist back to their naturally curly state. "You two again?"

"I'm terribly sorry to trouble you, Ms. Walters," said Lockhart, "but it's important that we speak. May we come in?"

Lockhart and Piper had spent the last hour with local police at the construction site, giving the authorities their version of what had gone down from the time Nick Castellano had shown up at Kristina Walters' apartment to when Lockhart had shot the man dead. Following a phone call to his chief of police, whom Lockhart had checked in with upon arriving in Roseburg, an on-scene officer told Lockhart and Piper they were free to go.

Now Kristina pivoted her head left to take in a soaking wet Piper. "What happened to you? You look like you jumped into a swimming pool with your clothes on."

"You're not far off," said Piper.

The dwelling's occupant opened the door, retreated

into her living room, and spun to face her guests, standing with her arms folded across her chest. "So, what is it this time?"

Piper trailed her boss into the apartment and then closed the door behind her.

Lockhart gave the late-twenties renter a shortened version of what had happened to Nick Castellano.

Kristina cursed. "I mean, I didn't exactly care for the guy, but I didn't want *that* to happen to him either." She cupped an elbow then held a palm to her mouth.

"I was hoping you could think back to your recent interactions with Castellano, specifically over the last week or so. Can you think of anything that seemed out of the ordinary? Did he act differently? Did he say anything that seemed odd?"

Piper shivered.

Kristina observed her female counterpart, almost feeling the other woman's discomfort herself. "I don't know." She paused. "I mean he wasn't really here all that much in the last week. Like I told you before, I haven't seen him since—" noticing Piper's body give off another violent shudder, she did a one-eighty, crossed the living room, and returned with a space heater. "Like I told you, I haven't seen him in the last three or four days."

"What about before that?" asked Lockhart.

She plugged in the heater, turned it toward Piper, then ducked into the bathroom, coming back a minute later with a couple of bath towels tucked under one arm.

She hooked a flimsy, wooden straight-back chair and dragged it across the floor, scooping a blanket from off the couch as she did so. "Here." She put the chair in front of the heater. "Sit down."

"Thanks, but I'm fine," said Piper.

Kristina sighed. "Girl, the deeper the cold sinks into your bones, the longer it takes for you to get warm." She motioned. "Sit."

Reluctantly, Piper sat.

The host laid the towels on Piper's lap then draped the blanket around her shoulders.

"Are you sure?" said Piper. "It's going to get all wet."

The stripper-hooker reluctantly envisioned what she had been doing a few hours earlier. "If there's one thing I've learned in life," a beat, "it's that everything comes clean in the wash."

Piper dialed up a grateful smile. "Thank you. I appreciate it."

"You're welcome," replied Kristina, before directing her attention toward Lockhart. "I'm sorry. What was your question again?"

"What about the days leading up to when you last saw Castellano? Do you remember anything that might tell us what he had been doing, or what he might have been planning to do?"

Kristina's chest swelled as she glanced away. Expelling a long breath, she faced him again while shaking her head. "Outside of him leaving my car a mess, we didn't see each other that much. I mean, he may have been here, but I never—"

Lockhart showed her a palm. "Hold up. You said he left your car a mess?"

She nodded. "He borrowed my car," she rolled her eyes toward the ceiling, "oh," a beat, "must've been a week ago now." She snapped her fingers and pointed at the sheriff. "It was the eighteenth. I'm sure of it. That was the start of me having the next three days off work. Since I had planned to hang around the apartment and get caught up on things, I didn't need the car. So, I told him, for a hundred dollars and a full tank of gas, he could use it."

Lockhart eyed Piper while running through the timeline in his head.

"The eighteenth was two days before Jace's murder," said Piper.

Lockhart regarded Kristina. "Would you mind if I searched your car?" He showed her his palms. "Whatever I find in there will not be held against you."

"Pfft," she retorted. "There's nothing illegal in my car." She pulled a set of keys from off a key rack beside the front door and handed them to the sheriff, quickly reclaiming them. "Wait. What if *he* put something illegal in there?"

"As an honorable man, and a representative of the law, you have my word, Ms. Walters, that nothing I find in there will come back on you."

"Yeah, it's that second part, the *law* part, I'm more worried about."

"I promise. I'm only interested in finding the man who murdered my son."

Her eyes grew bigger. "What did you say?" She shot a look at Piper then came back to Lockhart. "The cop who you said was murdered," a tick, "he was your son?" She eyed Piper.

Piper nodded.

Kristina faced Lockhart. "Oh, I didn't know. I'm so sorry." She touched fingertips to her lips then forfeited her keys. "Here. Feel free to turn it upside down if you need to."

"That won't be necessary, Ma'am."

"I'm truly sorry for your loss, Sheriff. I had no idea this was so personal for you."

Lockhart made his way toward the door.

Piper stood.

He pointed at her. "Stay and get warm."

"I should be with you."

"I think I can search a vehicle by myself." A pulse. "Stay here." He left.

Piper sat back down.

Kristina perched on the sofa's arm, six feet away from Piper, her gaze on the door. "I can't imagine what he's going through right now."

Piper studied the other woman, noticing genuine concern scrawled across her face in the form of squiggly forehead lines, sad eyes, and down-turned lips. Turning back to the heat, she scooted closer to the source of warmth before giving Kristina another glance. "Hey, listen." A moment. "I'm sorry for what I said earlier. I sometimes blurt out things before I've had a chance to think those things through."

Kristina frowned at the hunched over woman before recognition dawned on her face. *Always good to have multiple streams of income.* She waved off the apology. "Forget it. I got pissy with you, too. Sorry for cursing you out."

"I deserved it." A beat. "And you were still kind enough to," Piper glanced at the blanket, "give aid and comfort to the enemy."

"Well," Kristina sat on a couch cushion and crossed her legs at the knee, "we're not enemies anymore." A tick. "Can I get you something hot to drink, something to warm you up from the inside?"

"I have coffee in the truck, but I'm sure it's cold by now."

"I can whip up a cup of instant?"

"I wouldn't complain."

Kristina stood. "Be right back."

"Thank you...*again,*" said Piper.

"It's no trouble at all," replied the woman in the bathrobe while strolling into the kitchen.

• • •

Outside, Lockhart had spent the last fifteen minutes scouring Kristina's vehicle, an older model, four-door, blue Subaru Forester. He had begun his search in the rear cargo area and moved forward. Other than the seven paper bags, from different fast-food restaurants, strewn around the Subaru's backseat, and some dried mud on the front floor mats, the SUV was extremely clean.

Now sitting in the driver's seat, Lockhart flipped down visors, searched the glove box, center console, and the tiny overhead fold-down compartment near the rear-view mirror before using his flashlight to see under the front seats. Nothing. He heaved out a quick sigh while tapping his fingers on the steering wheel.

Thirty seconds later, he turned back toward the touchscreen on the dashboard and cocked his head. *I wonder.* He started the car and tapped the touchscreen, bringing up the Forester's onboard navigation system. A couple taps later, he was in the system's log. He scrolled up to the 18th and found one navigation route entered for that day.

Retrieving his notepad and pen, he jotted down the destination address listed, then reached behind him to grab the fast-food bags on the floor. He checked the receipts inside the bags and discovered all but one was from restaurants in the same town—Mesquite, Wyoming—the same town he had written moments ago. *Gotcha.*

•••

Ninety Minutes Later...

Back in Roseburg, Piper had used the address Lockhart had found on the Subaru Forester's navigation system to get the name of the person living at the address, Davis Bronson. Working with Wyoming authorities, she had gotten them to issue a statewide BOLO for Bronson, describing him as a man wanted for questioning in the murder of a Montana sheriff's deputy.

Then, after stripping off her blue jeans and jacket in her Dodge's backseat, and draping the clothing over the passenger seat's upright, Piper had stretched out under a wool blanket before knocking on the window above her head.

Having received the signal that she was decent, Lockhart had climbed behind the wheel. Wisely, he had taken off his leather jacket before starting their journey to Mesquite, Wyoming. Still, with the vehicle's air vents wide open, and the heat cranked up to 'high,' his blue denim button-up shirt had kept him quite warm, too warm. But that was a price he had happily paid to have his undersheriff dry and warm.

Now fully dressed and more rested, Piper was driving, poised to take her and Lockhart the rest of the way to Mesquite. She cocked her head while staring at the road ahead. "You know," a beat, "Tina's okay. I misjudged her. She's a kind girl who's had a tough life so far." Piper glimpsed Lockhart. "Did you know she used to work as a vet assistant," a tick, "and was studying to become a veterinary technician?" Piper turned back toward the road. "Until her life went to hell, that is."

"Tina?" asked Lockhart before returning to his task, taking stock of his remaining ammunition.

"Oh, that's right. You weren't there. You were searching her car. Kristina Walters?"

He nodded once.

"We actually got to know each other a little bit. As I said, she's nice," a beat, "and smart, too." Piper glimpsed him scowling at what he held, a full speedloader and two individual cartridges. "What's wrong?"

"We need to find an all-night gun store or some hardware store that sells ammo. I'm running low."

With the Ram 1500's cruise control set, Piper rolled onto her right hip, curled her right arm behind her seat, and dragged a duffle bag into the front compartment. "In here."

He eyed the black bag then did the same to her.

She saw him in her peripheral vision. "Just open it."

He placed the bag on his lap, ran the zipper, then spread the fabric. His eyes immediately spotted two 50-round boxes of the exact same brand of 44 Magnum ammunition he used. He faced her.

She lifted her right shoulder. "I figure if you're crazy enough to keep carrying a six-shot revolver in an age of fifteen, eighteen," she threw up an arm, "*twenty-round* semi autos, then I had better keep you well stocked with ammo. So, I started keeping a couple boxes of Maggies with my gear.”

While his features remained stoic, he couldn’t dispel the smile growing within him, “Thanks,” as he opened a flap on a box and started filling his speedloaders.

“You bet.”

ONE HOUR LATER
3:58 A.M.
SOUTH OF MESQUITE, WYOMING

Fifty-five minutes ago, after having reloaded his speedloaders and the ammo slide on his belt, Lockhart had reclined his seat and closed his eyes, telling Piper to wake him when they were fifteen minutes away from Mesquite.

Now, having awakened her boss ten minutes ago, Piper gave him a quick look. "So, do you think this Bronson guy is Jace's killer?"

"Don't know for sure." A beat. "Fast-food bags and an address in a navigation system aren't hard evidence of anything."

"Yeah, but still," she turned up her right palm, "it at least connects Castellano to Bronson. And based on Bartlett's testimony, Castellano was *in* the vehicle at the time of the murder."

"True;" replied Lockhart, "however, we don't know *what* the connection between those two men is. That's why we're questioning him."

Lost in thought, Piper nodded at the windshield.

"I'll tell you this, though," he wagged an index finger at her, "if Bronson *is* our killer, then he's going to be awfully skittish around law enforcement." A beat. "So, when we're talking to him, be ready to draw down on him."

She shook her head. "Don't need to…"

From inside a cup holder, Lockhart's phone vibrated.

"…tell me twice."

He answered. "Lockhart."

"Wade? Sheriff Tom Schneider here."

"What can I do for you, Sheriff?"

"It's more like what I can do for *you*. My office picked up some radio chatter coming out of Wyoming. Details are still sketchy, but it seems a sheriff's deputy from there got into a shootout during a traffic stop. He pulled over a man who he later discovered was the subject of a BOLO, one Davis Bronson."

Lockhart sat up straighter.

"What prompted me to call was the reason for the BOLO. Bronson is wanted for questioning in the murder of a—"

"A Montana sheriff's deputy," interjected Lockhart. "I know. My undersheriff issued that BOLO. We're five minutes away from Bronson's last known address. Where did this shootout take place?"

Piper whipped her head toward Lockhart, her eyebrows scrunched together. "Shootout?"

He held up a vertical index finger between him and her.

"Highway 191," answered Schneider, "south of

Yellowstone. The deputy is requesting backup, but the nearest responding LEO is an hour away."

"Do you have the deputy's coordinates?" Lockhart spun the 1500 SSV's terminal toward him then typed in what Schneider relayed to him. "Call the sheriff's office over there, Tom, and tell them two Montana sheriffs are in route. We're forty minutes away."

"I'm on it."

"Thanks for the call."

"Good luck and be safe, Wade."

Lockhart folded his phone in half.

"What's going on?" asked Piper.

"Bypass Mesquite and keep going north. We're responding to a call for help. A sheriff's deputy stopped a car belonging to Davis Bronson. Shots were fired, and we're the closest backup at forty minutes out."

Piper activated the Dodge's light bar and siren then let her right foot get heavy on the Ram's accelerator. "We'll be there in thirty."

...

Thirty Minutes Later...

Two thousand feet higher in elevation, the area north of Mesquite, Wyoming, was on the southern edge of an early-season snowstorm that was currently hammering the interior of Yellowstone National Park. Forecasters were predicting twelve inches in the next twelve hours.

What had been slush and rain in Roseburg was now an all-snow event in Mesquite; however, meteorologists were only calling for a few inches of the white stuff to fall on the less than five hundred residents in this area.

Having already shut off the Dodge's siren, Piper stopped the Ram behind an SUV, a black-and-white Ford Explorer, its lights flashing, its sides displaying the logo of the local sheriff's office.

Within seconds, Lockhart was out of the Dodge and down on one knee beside an injured deputy. "Where are you hit?"

Covered in snow and propped against the Explorer's left-rear tire, the late-twenties man grimaced, contorting his baby-faced, pudgy features. "Leg," he winced, "left one," before taking his left hand away from the right side of his stomach, "and here—ouch."

Carrying a first-aid kit and the wool blanket that had warmed her earlier, Piper dropped to both knees on Lockhart's left. The deputy was on his butt, his outstretched legs between his rescuers.

"He took off," the deputy lolled his head to his right, toward Yellowstone, "that way. The roads are closed up there, so if you hurry, you can—" he made a face, "you can still catch him."

"Negative, son," said Lockhart. "We're staying with you." While reading the young man's name plate on his uniform, FERGUS, he poked his chin at Fergus. "What's your name?"

"Deputy Fergus."

"Your *first* name."

"Jon."

"Jon, I'm Wade. This is Piper."

Fergus spied Piper.

After snapping on rubber gloves and opening the F/A kit, Piper dialed up a megawatt smile. "Hey there, Jon. Don't you worry one bit. We'll have you line dancing with your girlfriend in no time."

Lockhart began taking the supplies he needed from the red bag. "I'll take his leg."

She nodded while hauling out what she needed to tend to Fergus' belly wound.

Both worked quickly to stop the flow of blood.

Fergus' head came forward.

"Hey, hey, hey," said Piper. She cupped his chin and raised his head. "What are you doing? No going to sleep on me, you hear?"

He blinked a few times.

"Boy, I tell you." She worked, keeping one eye on her task and one on him. "You men are always going to sleep on me," she quipped. "What's with that, huh?"

He met her gaze.

She winked at him. "I'm starting to think there's something wrong with me."

Fergus lifted a corner of his mouth. "There's absolutely," he licked dry lips, "nothing wrong with you, Ma'am."

"Ma'am?" shot back Piper, a playfulness in her tone. "Are you saying I'm old?"

With Fergus' leg wound cleaned and bandaged, Lockhart twisted a long length of tape into thick 'string' and applied a makeshift tourniquet above the bullet hole.

"No, Ma'—" the deputy caught himself and smiled. "No, Miss Piper. I would nev—"

Treating Fergus' injury, Piper winced at the pain she had just inflicted on the young man. "I'm sorry, honey. I'm almost done. I promise." Seconds later, she applied a generous amount of tape to keep everything she had done in place then draped the wool blanket over him. Her job complete, she sat back on her haunches to wipe snow and sweat from her face with the sleeve of her jacket.

"You're going to be okay, son." Lockhart stood. "Help is on the way."

"I thought *you* were the help," said the deputy, his voice a couple notches above a whisper.

Lockhart turned his back on the other two and spoke into his phone. "Hey, Tom. Any idea on when the EMTs will be arriving." He lowered his voice further. "This kid's lost a lot of blood."

Overhearing her boss, Piper spun to sit on the pavement on Fergus' three o'clock. "Heck no, Jon. We're here to," she wrapped her left arm around his shoulders and held him, "to keep you company." She saw his eyelids drooping. "Hey. What did I say about closing your eyes? Let's play a game. How about rock-paper-scissors? Come on." She dug his right hand out from under the blanket. "Make a fist."

He lazily did as he was told.

"That's it. Good. Ready? You don't have to pump your hand." She pumped her hand with each number she counted off, "One, two, three," then stuck out her index finger.

Fergus slowly extended his first two fingers to make 'scissors.'

She pretended to write on his hand. "I win."

He scowled at her.

"What?" Piper held up her index finger. "It's a black marker. It writes on rocks, paper, scissors."

Despite his pain, Fergus half laughed.

"Okay, Tom. Thanks." Lockhart regarded Piper.

She saw the concern etched on his face.

He flashed five fingers at her three times.

She frowned at the side of Fergus' face, *Fifteen minutes*, before coming back to Lockhart.

Lockhart rolled his fore finger at her while mouthing the words, 'Keep him awake.'

Piper nodded. "All right, Jon. Let's go again. Make a fist for me, will you?"

He complied.

"Ready? One, two, three." After three pumps, she made a chopping motion, displaying a flat hand with her four fingers separated between the middle and ring finger, making what looked like a bigger pair of 'scissors.'

Fergus stuck out his index finger and mumbled, "I win. Black marker."

"Ah, but," Piper used her larger pair of 'scissors' to 'cut' his 'black marker,' "bolt cutters can cut through *everything*."

His amusement overtaking his pain, Fergus laughed. "You cheat."

"Cheat? Oh, wait. You probably think we're playing by the original rules, don't you?" She shook her head. "No, these are the new and improved rules we're playing by."

He rolled his eyes. "No more."

"Okay, let's play another game. Um...I see something," she paused, "I see something white. What am I seeing?"

"If you play this game like you did the," he wet his lips and swallowed, "the last one, how can I trust you'll be honest?"

"Oh, Jon. You're sharp. There's no getting anything past you, is there?"

Listening to Piper trying to keep Fergus awake and alive, Lockhart bypassed the two, ambled to the front of the cruiser, and stared at the road ahead, his mind envisioning himself catching up to Bronson. He wondered what he would do once his Ruger was within range of the monster who had most likely taken his son's life. Why else would he shoot a deputy and flee? The evidence against the suspect was mounting. Lockhart wiped snow from his face. He was ninety percent sure

Davis Bronson had gunned down Jace in cold blood. And Bronson would pay for that crime. How? Lockhart had not yet made that determination.

ONE HOUR LATER

Back at where the shootout had occurred, an ambulance had arrived, and the EMTs had worked feverishly to get the injured deputy stabilized, starting him on a pint of blood before getting him into the back of the ambulance. After one EMT had closed the back doors, she looked at Lockhart and Piper and said, "If you hadn't arrived when you did, and treated his wounds, we'd be taking away a corpse right now."

Then, while another deputy had been processing the scene, collecting evidence, Lockhart and Piper had excused themselves and driven north.

Now, walking away from a black, four-door BMW 3 Series sedan that had slid off the highway and was now in the weeds, stuck in snow, Lockhart followed footprints across the highway, Piper beside him. Both people stopped in the snow on the opposite side of the highway.

Lockhart shined his flashlight, a 6.2-inch-long Pelican 2360 and flooded the snow with 375 lumens and nearly 9,200 candelas. It didn't take long to spot the tracks leading off into the woods toward the west.

Piper took in trees that stood like telephone poles. A

fire had recently swept through here, leaving most everything leafless, including the trees that had fallen and were now haphazardly crisscrossing the terrain. Some areas had not been touched by the fire and were still 'green' and alive. In those areas that had been scorched, grasses, weeds, and scraggly shrubs had already returned. 'Pioneer trees,' mostly pines, were growing back, too. Yes, nature was hard at work, restoring the landscape. "Looks like he abandoned his car and is escaping on foot."

"Looks that way." Remembering his conversation with the sheriff of this small county, and how that sheriff had told him that a couple of his deputies were out of commission—in addition to Deputy Jon Fergus— Lockhart thumbed open his flip phone. "I need to make a phone call."

• • •

Ninety Minutes Later...
6:46 A.M.
More than an hour away from sunrise, the red, newer-model Jeep Wrangler Sport rolled to a stop behind the Dodge Ram 1500 SSV truck. At the wheel of the Wrangler, Sierra Courtright put the SUV's transmission in 'Park,' but left the vehicle running. After answering the call from Lockhart, she had made the drive up from her home in Justice, Wyoming.

In the beam of the Jeep's headlights, peering through

falling snow, Sierra zeroed in on Lockhart's backside and saw him with his hands on his hips and his head bowed as if he were praying. She pressed her lips together. *He's been through so much*, she thought. Losing a spouse at such a young age would be difficult for sure, but losing a son, too, and in such a violent, horrible manner?

She recalled her own trial in the wilderness in Upstate New York. While that incident had been terrifying, she at least had the satisfaction of knowing when the ordeal had ended. For Lockhart, he had to be carrying around his pain hour by hour, minute by minute, wondering when the sadness and the hurt would go away.

From experience, Sierra knew all too well that devastating events, traumatizing events, never really went away. Life went on. It had to. And in the quiet moments, when no one was around, when you're left with only your thoughts, bits and pieces of your painful past seeped out from the deepest recesses of your mind. It couldn't be helped. Over time, however, she had discovered a way to fight back against the forces weighing down her soul, the evil forces clawing at her, trying to pull her into bottomless pits of loneliness and despair.

She closed her eyes. *Lord Jesus, be with Wade. Help him to get through this. Give him strength to keep going, to keep living.* Sierra opened her eyes to see Lockhart pivot his head left and stare toward her. *Wade and I barely know each other, Jesus, so I understand if I'm not part of Your plan to save him, but,* she watched Lockhart turn and start strolling toward her, *but please send him someone who can get him on track again, someone who can help him start living again. Amen.*

Sierra filled her lungs and exhaled, her cheeks puffing outward, before she glanced in the rear-view mirror to see Ranger's broad head facing her. "Hang tight, Range. Be right back." After grabbing a red stocking cap, she opened her door, stepped out, and shut the door. Wearing a knee-length white winter coat, blue insulated skinny jeans, and black-and-brown, knee-high hiking boots that laced up the front, she donned her cap, stuffed hands into coat pockets, and hunched her shoulders against the cold. She met Lockhart beside the Dodge Ram's passenger side.

"Thanks again for coming," said Lockhart. "I hope I didn't start your day too early."

She smiled while whipping off a quick headshake. "I was already up. Ranger had to go out."

He gave her a quick visual checkup. "Are you sure you're feeling up to this? A few days ago, you were still getting tired halfway through the day."

"As you said, that was a few days ago. Yesterday, I felt almost like my old self. And today, after a full-night's sleep, I feel even stronger."

He nodded. "I'm glad to hear that."

Sierra gazed into his eyes and saw staring back at her, the same heavy eyes she had seen so many times in her bathroom mirror. He wasn't simply tired from work. No. He was battling demons. Her heart ached for him.

Lockhart reached into his pocket and retrieved a sealed plastic bag. Inside the see-through container was a large scrap of black leather. "I cut this from," he motioned, "the BMW over there. Do you think there's enough of a scent for Ranger to follow? I made sure to wear gloves when I cut it."

She claimed the bag and examined it before cranking her head left and right to peek at the surrounding woods. "You said you think you know which way he went?"

Lockhart stretched out his right arm toward his four o'clock. "His tracks lead west-northwest." A tick. "We figure he has almost a three-hour head start. Local law enforcement is stretched thin, so it's just us on this."

"Okay, well, I guess we'll see what happens when I give this to Ranger. Hopefully, he takes off in the same direction as your suspect did."

Piper came up and stood on her boss' two o'clock, Sierra's ten o'clock. "Hey, Sierra."

"Hi, Piper."

"Glad you made it." The undersheriff glanced at Sierra's lower abdomen before eyeing the woman. "How are you feeling?"

"Good to go."

"That's great. Can I get you anything?"

"Thanks, but," Sierra hooked a thumb over her shoulder, "I'm all packed with everything I should need."

She faced Lockhart. "When do we leave?"

"Whenever you're ready."

"I'll get Ranger then," she replied before heading toward her Wrangler.

Lockhart gave the wooded area a look, his mind calculating the probabilities of him having to take a long shot. "Wish I had thought to bring my Henry."

Digging out her keys, while meandering to the right side of the truck's bed, Piper unlocked the passenger side RamBox storage bin, hauled out a long gun, and held it out to him.

He accepted the Henry Big Boy Steel Side Gate lever action rifle before eyeballing its caliber—44 Magnum—as well as the black sleeve on the dark brown wooden buttstock's left side, the sleeve holding fourteen cartridges of 44 Magnum. This was his gun. And yet, this wasn't his gun. Lockhart frowned at Piper.

"Like I said before, if you're still crazy enough to be carrying around a lever gun, when there's no shortage of 30-round AR-15s, well, then..." she let her voice trail off.

"How long have you had this?"

She closed one eye. "Since shortly after I stopped trying to convince you to get an AR."

He did have an AR. He had many rifles in many calibers; however, his hand seemed to gravitate toward the Henry. It was plenty of gun for most criminal interactions in Big Sky County. Plus, he just loved lever guns.

Lockhart shouldered the Big Boy and pointed it at the pavement. "How is it sighted in," a tick, "pumpkin on the fence or—"

"Nope. Just put the front bead where you want the bullet to go. I sighted it in for the load you usually carry." Piper pointed at the magazine tube. "It's fully loaded, but the chamber's empty."

Turning his back on her, he ran the lever, eased the hammer down, then plucked a cartridge from the ammo sleeve to top off the gun. "These aren't cheap. How much do I owe you?"

"Nothing." Piper closed and locked the RamBox. "As you so clearly pointed out to me earlier," she slapped 'her' truck twice, "the taxpayers also own," then aimed a finger at the Henry, "*that.*"

He faced her, recalling how he had informed her that her truck didn't truly belong to *her.*

She lifted a corner of her mouth.

He pursed his lips and nodded. "Touché."

Pleased, she nodded back at him. "Thank you."

With his right hand holding the gun by the receiver, down by his right thigh, he regarded her. "I was planning to surprise you, but then," shaking his head, his demeanor sunk, "but then everything happened, and I got a little," he ran the back of his left hand across his chin, "well, you know."

Piper leaned back against her truck.

"Anyway, I'm planning to put your name in for a

raise.”

She spied him. “Really?”

“You’ve been with me for six years now, and outside of your cost-of-living increases, you’ve never had a pay raise. All the paperwork is ready. I just have to submit it, which I’ll do at the next board meeting. There shouldn’t be any pushback. If there is, I’ll push back *harder*. You’re a good undersheriff, and you deserve a paycheck that reflects how much you mean to me—*this office*.”

Piper grinned, partly at the thought of her pay increase, but more at his attempt to cover up his ‘how much you mean to me’ faux pas. “Thanks, Wade. I appreciate that.”

Lockhart saw Sierra and Ranger approaching, Ranger decked out in a harness with a leash running from the yoke to her hand. He came back to Piper. “No need to thank me. You’ve *earned* it.”

With a backpack slung over her shoulder, Sierra stopped a few feet away from Big Sky’s top two LEOs. “We’re ready.”

Lockhart nodded then slung his rifle over his right shoulder.

“Let’s do this,” said Piper.

“Ranger, on me,” said Sierra.

The German Shepherd dog sat facing her.

“Time to work, boy.”

The dog stood, his tail wagging.

She opened the plastic bag and held it in front of

him.

He stuck his snout inside and sniffed the leather article.

She then closed the bag, let out more of his leash, and said, "Seek, Ranger. Seek!"

The dog immediately scampered back and forth, his nose to the ground. He went to the BMW and sniffed the seat from where the scent article had been cut. He hopped into the car and sniffed the seat's upright before jumping down and zigging and zagging away from the BMW. His nose to the ground, he followed the same path Lockhart and Piper had taken earlier. Only this time, Ranger headed into the woods, bounding over fallen trees, rounding upright trunks, and bypassing small shrubs. There was no trail to follow. The falling snow and blowing wind had covered up any tracks Bronson had made. So, Ranger made his own path.

Drawing in her dog's leash, so it didn't get caught on branches, Sierra followed, Lockhart and Piper on her 'six.'

"How do we know he's going the right way?" asked Piper. "There aren't any tracks to follow."

"He's not following tracks," said Sierra. "He's got your suspect's scent."

Frowning, Piper spied Lockhart.

Lockhart glimpsed his undersheriff. "Ranger's cross trained in trailing and air scent detection."

Her frowned deepened.

"He's not following Bronson's *tracks*. He's following the man's *scent*. And that scent could be anywhere—the ground, leaves, brush, or the wind itself.

"Okay," she replied. "If you say so." A beat. "So, what are *we* supposed to do?"

"We let," Lockhart motioned ahead of him, "*them* lead us to Bronson."

"And if Ranger's nose starts following a bunny rabbit?"

"That's all part of the relationship between handler and dog. Right now, she's reading Ranger's actions, making sure he hasn't jumped scents."

"Sounds complicated."

Sierra tossed a quick glance over her left shoulder, "Trust me, Piper," then faced forward again. "Ranger and I have done this many times. I know my dog."

8:05 A.M.

Since being shot while rescuing Sierra from her abductor years ago, Ranger couldn't trail for much more than an hour at a time. Any longer, and he was sure to start limping. If it were up to him, however, he would have dragged his bad leg along until he found whatever he was seeking for his handler.

Sierra checked her watch and saw they had been trailing for an hour and fifteen minutes. She studied the landscape and noted the slope was getting steeper. So far, the land behind them had been fairly level, and there were not nearly as many fallen trees to contend with now as there had been when the journey had begun—the recent fire that had burned what was behind them had spared the land ahead. So, she had felt confident in letting Ranger continue. But with the way ahead becoming more vertical, it was time to stop. "Ranger, come."

The dog came to her and sat facing his owner.

"Good boy." She patted him then unhooked the leash from his harness. "Break."

Ranger went to all fours and sniffed the ground while moving around the area. He lifted his leg and peed on a pine seedling before continuing his inspection.

"He needs to rest." Sierra slid her backpack off her shoulders and sat on a horizontal log.

Lockhart sat on her left while propping his rifle against the log on his nine o'clock.

Catching her breath, watching Ranger go from one spot to another, Piper claimed 'real estate' on the wood on Sierra's right before taking a swig of water from one of the two bottles she had stowed in her jacket pocket.

Likewise, Sierra and Lockhart drank from their own bottles.

"So, Sierra," Piper capped her bottle, peeped at the woman she was addressing, then continued to watch Ranger, "how many of these," she wavered, "these hunts, for lack of a better term, have you and Ranger been on, anyway?"

"Gosh," Sierra arched her brows, "I'd have to go back and count them all up, but," she paused, "maybe close to two dozen. We've only been doing this for two years, though, and I have no clue if two dozen is a lot or not."

"Well, you've logged two from *us* in the last month, so..."

Piper and Sierra shared a laugh.

"Tell me about you," prompted Sierra. "Wade says you spent time in New York, too?"

Lockhart tipped his water bottle back again, content to let the women chat, get to know each other a little better. He wasn't interested in talking, anyway. His mind had slipped over to thinking about his son. At twenty-four, with his whole life ahead of him, a life—and a career—full of promise, Jace had been snuffed out at what should have been a simple traffic stop. Sierra's voice broke his train of thought.

"Ranger, come," said Sierra.

The dog ran to her.

"Down."

The dog laid on his left side, next to her boots, his head close to her, and Lockhart's, footwear.

She patted him. "Take it easy for a few minutes."

"I can't believe how well-behaved he is," commented Piper.

"They're intelligent dogs to begin with, and if you train them well, and maintain their training, they'll give you no problems."

"Question," said Piper. "Has he ever *not* found whatever it was you wanted him to find?"

"Never."

Piper cocked her head at Sierra. "Really?"

"Yup. He's..."

Lockhart's mind drifted back to his son. A few moments later, he thought of Davis Bronson; specifically, the investigation that had led Lockhart to this point. As long as he had something to focus his energy toward, Lockhart could keep his emotions over Jace's murder at bay; however, at times like these, when his mind relaxed, he couldn't help but think about what he would do when he caught up with Bronson.

Ranger scooted closer to Lockhart to sniff the man's boots.

Lockhart poured water into his cupped palm.

The GSD lapped it up.

Still conversing with Piper, Sierra saw him out of the corner of her eye and half smiled to herself.

Pouring more water, Lockhart thought of the two paths he was on. Depending on what he was doing, one kept him focused on catching his prey while the other had him wrestling with his anger; in this instance, anger being code for revenge.

Ranger licked Lockhart's palm dry for a third time then turned away.

Stroking the dog's neck, intermittently scratching at the base of Ranger's ears, Lockhart scowled. He knew his two paths were on a collision course. The first one was bound to happen. He would not rest until he apprehended Davis Bronson; however, how would the second path tie into the first? What was he going to do to Bronson? Lockhart didn't know. And that scared the hell out of him. How can you lead a sheriff's office when the sheriff breaks the law?

A minute later, Lockhart patted Ranger on the shoulder then sat tall, his eyes scanning the way ahead. *I guess I'll battle that beast when it rears its head.*

•••

Twenty Minutes Later...

Having resumed the search for Bronson, with the wind having died to a breeze an hour ago, and the snow stopping altogether, Sierra now noticed Ranger had been following faint tracks in the snow, tracks that led toward the northwest.

Ranger strayed to his left, his nose pointed upward, before he returned to the indentations. A few strides later, he veered left again while sniffing the wind.

Lockhart also noticed the dog's behavior.

Fifty feet later, Ranger made an abrupt left and began trailing toward the southwest.

"Sierra?" prompted Lockhart.

"I'm not sure." She tugged on the leash a bit.

Ranger tugged back, his body pointing toward the southwest.

Piper glimpsed the clearly visible footprints in the snow then surveyed the area to the southwest to see a dense forest and rolling hills in the distance. No snow had fallen in this area. If she squinted, she could make out a clearing in a valley between two large tree stands. "Has he lost the scent?"

"No. In fact, I think he's picking up an even stronger one." Sierra faced Lockhart. "It's your call, but Ranger is telling us we need to turn to the south."

"Wait a minute," Piper interjected. "The tracks lead," she gestured toward the northwest, "*that* way. Why does he want to go *away* from them?"

"The wind," said Lockhart, feeling a breeze coming out of the south-southwest. He sought confirmation from Sierra, who nodded at him. He scratched his right cheek while looking to the north. "It's the snowstorm that's burying Yellowstone right now." He pointed in the direction the tracks were going toward. "Bronson must've headed into the teeth of it. Then, somewhere up there, he turned back and started going south, away from the storm."

"We don't *know* if he did that, Wade," said Piper.

Sierra eyed her dog. "*Ranger* knows," a beat, "well, at least he knows where we should be going."

Piper raised a hand toward the other woman, "No offense, but," before directing the same hand, her palm turned skyward, toward the tracks in the snow, "we have visible proof Bronson went *that* way. For all we know, he could've stayed on the edge of the storm and is way up there. If we turn south and end up going the wrong way, we'll never make up that ground."

Lockhart mulled over her argument for the next few seconds.

Sierra shrugged. "That's for you two to decide. Ranger and I are only here to offer our assistance."

Piper faced Lockhart, who was still analyzing the landscape. "Wade?"

Squinting, he stroked his chin then met his undersheriff's steely gaze before going from Ranger to Sierra. "What if you let him sniff the scent article again?"

Sierra opened the bag.

Ranger sniffed.

"Seek, Ranger. Seek!" commanded Sierra.

The dog put his nose to the ground and bolted toward the tracks in the snow.

"See?" A pleased Piper lifted an arm. "I told y—"

Ranger did a one-eighty, raised his nose, then took off toward the southwest.

Piper's shoulders sagged. "Aw, crap."

Sierra followed her dog. "What are we doing here, people? Do I pull him back or what?"

Lockhart regarded his second-in-command.

Observing his facial features, Piper saw he had already made his decision, so she didn't challenge him. Instead, she let out a sigh before traipsing after Sierra and Ranger. "You know, in the academy, they said to follow *evidence, clues*. They never told us to," she huffed out a cloud of water vapor, "*follow the wind.*"

With dark storm clouds still hovering above Yellowstone to the north, the skies to the south were overcast, but clearing here and there to allow a low sun to poke out from time to time. For the first hour, after having turned to the southwest, Lockhart had noticed Ranger was veering more and more southward, changing his path every fifteen or twenty minutes. He and Sierra had concluded that Bronson had been walking due south while Ranger's nose had been leading the trio on a gradually curving, intersecting course, one that was gaining ground on their target.

Following another rest period, Ranger had spent the last hour on a due south path. He had never strayed left or right once, making it clear to everyone that they were now directly behind their suspect. How far behind? With Bronson doubling back, and Ranger following the man's scent, and not his tracks, Lockhart had figured that alone had shaved at least an hour off the man's three-hour head start. Throw in Bronson taking a couple 15-minute rest breaks himself, maybe longer if the fugitive felt confident that no one was chasing him, and Lockhart had estimated they were no more than an hour behind, maybe less if their pace had been quicker than Bronson's.

After another rest break, the tracking party had been following Ranger for the last forty-five minutes, emerging from the forest to traverse a stretch of open land before entering another wooded area. This one, however, hadn't been as dense. There had been room to maneuver among the trees. Plus, they had been on what seemed like a hiking trail. The earth was matted, as if many backpackers had been down this trail.

Now, coming out from the cover of the tree canopy, Ranger led the way across an old wooden bridge that crossed a flowing stream filled with boulders ranging in size from basketballs to truck tires. Rising three feet above the water, the crossing was made of eight-inch-diameter round logs that ran perpendicular to the stream. Thick and wide planks ran parallel to the water and made up the walkway's surface. Even though it was worn, it still appeared to be structurally sound.

On the other side of the twenty-foot expanse, the edge of the stream met up with an embankment of evergreens, naked leafy trees, small and large shrubbery, weeds, and even a few wildflowers. The main eye-catcher, however, were the massive boulders and outcroppings. Some were completely above ground. Others were embedded into the hillside, foliage and trees disguising portions of them, so their true size was unknown.

Stepping onto the bridge, with Piper a half step ahead of him and on his eleven o'clock, Lockhart glanced both ways along the stream.

To his right were trees lining the banks of the water. On his four o'clock, the land rose sharply to join with a shaded mountain range that ran west-southwest, the distant peaks lit up by a sun that had yet to crest the crag on his eight o'clock.

To his left, more trees ran along the bubbling waters. Bigger boulders on the stream bed forced the water to find another way around them. A distant mountain range to the south, running parallel to the one behind Lockhart, was bathed in sunshine with several stands of tall spruces, cedars, and pines positioned along its slopes. The sound of tumbling waters carried a peacefulness that, if left unchecked, threatened to sweep Lockhart away from the gravity of his task. Up ahead, further up the slope, the gurgling croaks, each rising in pitch, from several ravens calling out to each other raced downhill to shake him from his short-lived respite.

Blending in almost perfectly with the surrounding terrain, a brown patch behind a motorcycle-sized rock, fifty yards away on his nine o'clock, caught Lockhart's attention. Over the years, his trained eye had spotted many such patches like this one. The shape moved, and antlers rose above the rock as two black eyes gaped toward him and his companions, water dripping from the buck's mouth. In his head, Lockhart counted. *One, two, three,* he squinted, *four, five,* a beat, *eight points.* Seconds later, the stag whirled around and bounded away, its white tail disappearing into the underbrush.

Reaching the far side of the bridge, Ranger stopped. He raised his nose toward the south before jerking his head toward the southwest, toward the search party's two o'clock. In the next instant, he cocked his head, his ears standing straight up.

Lockhart squinted at the dog's stance then pivoted his head toward the southwest. He saw nothing but land, rocks, and trees. But something inside him came alive as a chill raced up his spine.

Ranger let out a low growl before he moved forward to the end of his leash.

Sierra noticed her dog's hackles had gone up. "Uh, Wade?"

Lockhart bolted across the bridge, grabbing Piper by the right elbow.

A single gunshot cut through the valley, its report bouncing off boulders.

A bullet skipped off a plank behind Lockhart.

Splinters flew into the air.

"Go," he said. "Get to that ledge."

Piper ran to the end of the bridge and leaped over a rock on her left before ducking behind the ledge he had indicated.

Ranger barked wildly, his tail wagging, saliva dripping from his chin.

Sierra darted ahead.

Lockhart wrapped his left arm around her waist,

"This way," then pulled her off the bridge to his right, both jumping to the ground two feet below before dropping to their sides behind another low projection.

Ranger barked.

"Ranger, come," commanded Sierra.

The GSD came to her.

She grabbed him by his harness and dragged him to the ground between her and Lockhart.

Multiple gunshots rang out a split-second before bullets clipped twigs or ricocheted off stone above their heads.

Lying on his right side, facing Sierra, Lockhart glimpsed Piper on the opposite side of the bridge. She had drawn her Glock and was peeking out from cover. He spied Sierra, who was examining Ranger. "Is everyone okay?"

"I'm good," replied Piper.

"I'm okay," said Sierra before glancing up at him while patting her dog twice on the shoulder. "He's good, too."

"Ranger," Piper glimpsed the dog, "it would seem apologies are in order. I'll never doubt you again." She stuck her head up then quickly ducked again. "Wade, I think he's behind a rock a hundred feet away. To our right. One to two o'clock position."

Having unslung his Henry Big Boy, Lockhart now rolled onto his back and held the gun in his hands, muzzle pointing up the slope. He removed his Resistol hat, placed it beside Sierra, then filled his lungs. "Davis Bronson," he yelled. "Sheriff Lockhart. Big Sky County. You're under arrest for the murder of one of my deputies. Drop your weapons and come out with your hands up."

Five seconds passed.

From higher up, a man's voice: "Don't think so, Sheriff. Montana has the death penalty. And I prefer to go out on *my* terms, not strapped to a table or some chair." Bronson punctuated his words by sending a round into the rock above Lockhart's head.

Lockhart and Sierra 'turtled' their heads.

"He definitely has a bead on our position," remarked the sheriff before he surveyed his surroundings. The stream was essentially a wall. There was no way to cross it without getting shot. And the bridge to his right was too exposed. Even the land above them, to the south, had no cover between the crossing and the outcroppings further up the hillside.

"What are we going to do, Wade," said Piper. "We can't stay here."

Pondering his options, he gave the terrain another scan before cranking his head backward while envisioning the nearest outcropping. "Piper."

"Yeah?"

"Just like at that construction site," he kept his voice low, so Bronson couldn't hear him, "I'll keep his head down while you get to that first rock up the hill."

She peeked above the ledge in front of her, saw a rock

fifty feet away, then dropped low again. "Okay."

"When I start firing, you start running."

Piper nodded.

"Count my shots. When you get to ten, if you still haven't made it to that rock, make yourself thin."

"Are you telling me I'm fat?"

"*Thinner* then," he shot back before eyeing Sierra. "You two stay put and out of the fight, okay?" Reaching inside his coat, "But just in case this goes south," he drew his Ruger.

She put her hand on the gun, "No need," then drew a Smith & Wesson Shield Plus from a belt holster on her right side. "Based on my first 'S' and 'R' with you," 'Search and Rescue,' "I thought it best to bring my *own* this time."

"Very good." He holstered his Ruger then rolled away from her.

She grabbed his jacket.

He trundled back her way.

"I know it's stupid to say this, since I know you *will* be, but," she took in his sky-blue eyes, his long eyelashes, his hair, his strong features, "be careful, will you?"

Lockhart nodded once then army crawled away from her, staying below his cover as he worked his way along the bank of the stream. After snaking around and over sharp rocks, going as far as he dared, he went to his right shoulder to assume a firing position, the barrel of his Big Boy rifle poking out from behind two volleyball-sized pointed stones. He eyed Piper.

She went to a crouch before nodding that she was ready.

Lining up the Henry's sights with where he thought Bronson was, Lockhart fired his first shot, worked the lever, then fired again.

• • •

Fifteen Seconds Later...

Eight. Huffing and puffing, bent over, Piper dug the toes of her boots into the steep hill, her eyes on an enormous boulder fifteen feet away.

To her right, on her four o'clock, Lockhart let loose with another 44 Magnum.

Nine. Piper bent at the knees and ascended another three feet. *Not gonna make it.*

Boom!

She laid out flat, holding her Glock in her right hand and aiming to her right, her eyes flitting left and right, her brain searching for something to shoot at.

• • •

After firing his eleventh shot, Lockhart flipped over his Henry, so the loading gate on the right side of the gun was pointing skyward. One after the other, he plucked cartridges from the buttstock ammo carrier and fed them into the magazine tube under the gun's barrel.

From up the rise, nine-millimeter reports came at a steady clip.

He hunched down, expecting incoming rounds. But nothing came his way. Two beats later, he heard more nine-millimeter gunshots. These were coming from the bridge.

•••

Five Seconds Earlier...

Popping her head up from behind her cover, Sierra raised her brows at what she saw. Off to her right, a pistol was sticking out from behind a huge rock, the gun's muzzle rising and falling with each shot.

To her left, Piper was flat on her stomach, her left arm covering her head as incoming bullets tore up the ground around her.

Sierra brought her Smith & Wesson on target and fired at the pistol.

•••

Noticing the cessation of projectiles coming her way, Piper raised her head to see Sierra laying down her own covering fire. Piper got to her feet and made a mad dash for the rock, ten feet away.

ALEX ANDER   143

The slide on Sierra's Shield locked to the rear. Seeing Piper dive behind a rock, Sierra dropped to her butt, ejected her weapon's spent magazine, then loaded a full one.

With his Henry topped off, and noticing his girlfriend, as well as his undersheriff, safely behind cover, Lockhart scrambled to his feet and ran diagonally up the hill and to his right, stopping behind a wide tree trunk fifty feet from where he had just been. Facing the tree, he looked further upward and picked out another wide trunk thirty feet away.

Backing away from his cover, with the Big Boy pressed into his left shoulder, Lockhart leaned right and fired at where Bronson was holed up. Working the lever and firing as he moved, he trudged upward. Seven rounds later, he put his back to an oak. With his Henry pointing upward, he ran the lever up and down with his left hand before pulling the last two cartridges from the rifle's buttstock ammo sleeve and feeding them, along with five rounds from the ammo slide on his belt, past the gun's loading gate.

Lockhart twisted his head counterclockwise, his

upper body following, to see around the oak's trunk, to see the rock formation that was concealing Bronson. The man had not gotten off a round, since Sierra had reigned down a full mag on the guy. *Could be injured. Or dead*, he thought. Didn't matter. Either way, he needed to get eyes on the man.

After glancing once more toward Bronson's position, Lockhart pushed himself away from the tree and ran toward the start of a stand of conifers. They weren't cover, but they at least offered him some concealment. If he was quiet, maybe he could take Bronson by surprise.

Entering the stand, Lockhart carefully picked his way through the mini forest. Avoiding fallen pinecones, he tiptoed over a bed of brown needles. If his bearings were correct, he had managed to get behind Bronson's last known position.

Ten steps later, he bypassed a shrub before peeking through a gap in the forest to see Piper aiming her gun at him. She quickly lowered it. Having taught her hand signals, hand signals he had learned from his days in the military, he now used those gestures to tell her what he was going to do.

Piper nodded.

Lockhart rounded an eight-foot Douglas fir. With its well-shaped and filled-out branches, it would have been a perfect Christmas tree for the family room in any home. His left shoulder grazed the tree's boughs as he slipped by it, charged out into the open, and leveled his rifle at nothing. He quickly swung the long gun upward and to the right, his eyes scanning for his two-legged predator. He backed up to where shiny brass cases lay in two small groups on the ground. Sounding like a bird, he whistled.

Ten seconds later, Piper came into view ten feet from him, holding her Glock 19 at the low-ready position. She saw the cases then aimed her gun upward, searching for Bronson. "Where is he?" she whispered. "He never passed by me."

Lockhart used his boot to flip over an empty black magazine near the rock. "Looks like he's using a full-size Taurus. Nine-millimeter. Seventeen-round magazines. And I count," several beats, "thirty cases here."

She whipped her head toward the magazine and the cases then went back to looking for Bronson. "Thirty that you can *see*. Those buggers have a knack for finding the tiniest of hiding places." Piper swung her gun left, "Maybe he's out of ammo," before swinging the weapon to the right.

"Or into a third mag," countered the sheriff.

She glimpsed him, "Three? Really?" before returning to her search for Bronson. "A lot of concealed carriers don't even pack a *single* spare." A pulse. "So, what now?"

Lockhart dipped his head to try to spot tracks on the ground, but there were too many needles. He looked up and around before motioning straight up the hill. "Go that way. I'll go right."

With her pistol leading the way, she climbed the

slope.

"Watch yourself, Piper."

"You too."

AMBUSH

Lockhart pushed through some brush, then ducked under a low branch, before coming to a stretch of level ground nestled between a dozen towering evergreens to his left, further up the grade, and the top halves of trees from down the grade on his right. Up ahead, both large and small outcroppings were positioned close together, leaving a narrow, winding 'alleyway' among the projections. And most of those projections were taller than he was. Finally, smaller, 'holiday' sized pines and scraggly bushes were scattered among the substantial boulders and flat ledges, making it difficult to see what lay ahead.

Lockhart crept into the alleyway. His senses were heightened. His heart was beating harder. With his lever gun in both hands and pulled deep into his left shoulder, he kept swinging the muzzle left and right while snaking around rock faces, trees, and shrubs, the tops of some overhangs gradually coming into view with each step.

Behind him: Something hit the forest floor.

He whirled left, leading with the Henry.

A second later, a rustling sound came from somewhere up above.

He raised the rifle, his eyes scanning for Bronson, his mind suggesting the man had climbed a tree and was waiting to ambush him. A tick later, he spotted a squirrel higher up.

The brown squirrel let go of something and scurried along a branch.

The husk of a nut hit the ground with a light thud two seconds afterward.

From his six o'clock, a heavy force slammed into Lockhart. It started at his left shoulder blade then spread to between his shoulder blades and down the middle of his back. Rotating clockwise, his body was thrown forward. He took his right hand off the Henry to break his fall. Tumbling and rolling, he tried to go with the motion.

The rifle was ripped from his grasp.

Two rolls later, now on his back, he got his bearings and looked up to see Davis Bronson staring down at him.

Straddling his enemy's hips, Bronson leaned forward and sent out a right cross.

Lockhart turned away, but his left cheek ended up absorbing most of the punch.

The outlaw came down with another 'right.'

The sheriff got his left arm in the way and partially deflected the blow.

Bronson rocked his upper body backward, prepping for another strike.

With his right hand, Lockhart grabbed Bronson's belt

buckle, his fingers slipping inside the man's waistband. Using his opponent's weight against him, Lockhart wrenched on the buckle while sliding his body further between Bronson's legs.

Being jerked forward, Bronson reached out with both arms to keep from face planting.

Rolling onto his left hip, Lockhart coiled his arms around the man's right arm and buckled Bronson's same elbow with a hard left forearm before sweeping Bronson's right hand off the earth.

The criminal went crashing onto his right side.

Lockhart got to his knees, pinned his attacker to the ground, and nailed him with three rapid-fire left crosses.

The prone man's nose cracked on the second strike.

Blood poured out of Bronson's nostrils.

Winded, Lockhart was slow to cock his arm.

Bronson took advantage of the delay and shot out two jabs to Lockhart's chin before lifting his legs and kicking the lawman off him.

Lockhart fell backward.

Bronson rolled onto his stomach, spotted the Henry Big Boy six feet away, then scrambled after the long gun.

Lockhart caught the man's right foot, dug in his heels, and dragged Bronson away from the 44 Magnum.

Bronson rotated his body clockwise, drew his left knee to his chest, and thrust out his boot.

Lockhart hunched his right shoulder and diverted the kick before plucking something clipped to his right-front jean pocket.

Bronson raised his knee again and drove his left foot toward Lockhart's face.

Pinwheeling his right arm, Lockhart redirected the man's left leg outward then, with a flick of his right wrist, he opened his Buck 110 Hunter Sport knife, assumed a reverse grip, his thumb on the end of the handle, and sunk the 3.75-inch blade into the criminal's inner left thigh.

Bronson threw his head back and howled in pain. He laid out flat, his head hitting the ground, as he grabbed for his bleeding leg.

In a flash, Lockhart was on him, straddling him, down on his left knee, his right Ariat boot beside Bronson's left shoulder. Clutching clothing with his left hand, he reared back with his right fist and broke the man's nose a few more times. Breathless, his muscles working on pure adrenaline, he threw back the right half of his jacket, yanked out his Ruger, and jammed the weapon's more-than-one-inch-diameter barrel, front sight and half underlug included, into his son's murderer's mouth, breaking an incisor and a canine in the process. "Time for justice, you sick son-of-a—"

"Wade!"

Recognizing Piper's voice, he didn't turn toward her. Instead, he just kept glaring at the one who had gunned down his deputy, his only son. "Walk away, Piper." He grabbed a few gulps of air. "This doesn't concern you anymore."

Choking on the 4.2 inches of steel filling his mouth and pressing against the back of his throat—as well as his own blood and broken teeth—Bronson struggled to free himself.

Lockhart cocked the Ruger's hammer.

The outlaw stopped squirming, knowing any movement now against the Redhawk's single-action trigger pull could release the gun's hammer.

"I can't do that," said Piper, her Glock 19 in hand, hanging down by her right hip. "I'm here. I'm involved."

His left hand driving a ball of clothing up into Bronson's throat, Lockhart spoke through clenched teeth, "He killed Jace," before his chest heaved outward.

"I know."

All the oxygen left his lungs in one gust, "He killed my *son*!" as spittle shot out of his mouth.

"I know. I know. And he'll pay," a beat, "in a court," she shook her head, "but not here, not like this, Wade."

Lockhart gripped the Hogue Monogrip as hard as he could, the revolver shaking in his hands. "I told you. Walk. Away."

"Don't do this to me. If you pull that trigger, I'll have to arrest you for murder or quit my job. And I don't want to do either one of those things." Piper inched to within three feet of her boss. Now standing on his nine o'clock, "Please," she lowered her voice to a whisper. "Don't make me choose."

His breaths came in short, swift gasps as he stared into the dark eyes of a killer, his right index finger tightening.

Piper laid her left hand on his left shoulder.

Lockhart felt the pressure, and something stirred inside him. He didn't know what it was, or where it had come from, but his desire to kill began to fade. His anger had never been more real than it was right now, but his drive for revenge was not as strong as it had been only a few seconds earlier.

"It's okay, Wade. You don't have to do this."

Shutting his eyes, he took a deep breath, then exhaled. In the next instant, after taking a hot-air-balloon-sized breath, he let out a guttural yell while jerking the Redhawk from Bronson's mouth and sending six rounds into the dirt on his three o'clock, his finger working the trigger three more times as the gun just 'clicked' on spent primers. Raising the nearly three-pound gun above his head, he slammed the muzzle into Bronson's face, opening a two-inch gash.

Before he could unleash another pistol-whip, Piper hooked his arm and hauled him off the prisoner. "Come on, Wade. It's okay. It's all over now."

His energy spent, he went with her to the ground, him on his back, her on her knees on his left. He stared up at the sky through breaks in the trees overhead.

The clouds had parted, and a bright-blue sky had appeared.

Feeling a lone teardrop creeping down over his left temple, he heard Piper's words again. *It's okay. It's all over now.* He swallowed, an image of Jace in the forefront of his mind, before closing his eyes. *No. It's not okay. And I fear it'll never be okay.*

Piper left him to secure Bronson.

Moments later, something rough gently slapped at his left cheek repeatedly.

Lockhart opened his eyes to make out a dark, furry outline silhouetted against the blue sky.

…

Minutes Later…

Sierra rounded an outcropping to see Piper handcuffing Bronson. She looked right to see Lockhart flat on his back and Ranger on all fours beside him.

Piper stood tall and spotted the terror on Sierra's face. She quickly waved her hands at the woman. "No, no. He's okay. Nothing happened to him. He's fine."

Sierra rushed toward Lockhart and kneeled beside his left thigh. With Ranger on her right—the GSD busy licking a cut under the prone man's left eye—and Piper on her seven o'clock, Sierra pulled on Ranger's leash. "Ranger, down."

The dog laid down before resting his snout on the sheriff's left shoulder.

"He went nuts when he heard you yell. Broke away

from me and charged up the mountain." Not getting a reaction, Sierra leaned forward and hovered above Lockhart.

The lawman gaped at the sky.

"Wade?" A pulse. "Wade."

He said nothing.

She gave him a few seconds then put a hand on each of his upper arms. "Talk to me, Wade."

He blinked a few times, glimpsed her, then went back to staring at the sky. "I wanted to kill him. I had the gun in my hand. The hammer was back. All I had to do was apply a few more pounds of pressure." Lockhart shut his eyes for the next few moments. "Then this feeling, this," he opened his eyes, "this awareness came over me. I don't know what it was. Maybe it was what people call a still, small voice. I don't know, but," he paused, "but this *voice* made me question if I was doing the right thing. And at that moment, all the drive to kill just," he wavered, "it just left me."

Sierra half smiled. "I'm glad you listened to that voice. No man is worth losing your soul over."

Having used Bronson's belt as a tourniquet for the man's knife wound, Piper got him on his feet and started walking him away from Lockhart and Sierra.

Lockhart rose to a sitting position and watched the hobbling man leave. "Now, however, I'm not so sure." He barely shook his head, still observing Bronson. "I'm not sure I made the right choice."

TWO MONTHS LATER
6:27 P.M.

Lockhart closed the front door to his house and stomped his feet on a coarse mat just inside the doorway, shaking snow from his boots. The white stuff was coming down in big flakes, and his black leather jacket was speckled with it. If the first week of January was any sign of how the rest of the month would play out, then Big Sky was about to see near record snowfall totals.

After giving his jacket a shake, he tossed the garment onto the mahogany-colored leather sofa that sat centered in the living room, facing the home's eight-foot-wide front window. A five-foot-long, dark oak, mission-style coffee table was sandwiched between the sofa and two leather lounge chairs that matched the sofa, their backs to the wide window. Behind the lounge chairs was a four-foot sofa table displaying family pictures. Area rugs were strategically placed over the space's polished hardwood floor.

To the rear of the sofa was a narrow brick wall that had a built-in fireplace. The fireplace was directly behind the three-person couch. In the southeast corner, to the left of the fireplace, where the bricks met up with a wood-paneled wall, sat a four-foot-wide oak gun cabinet that rose to within a foot of the room's nine-foot ceiling, a ceiling that sported crosshatched wooden beams to produce a 'chessboard appearance' of three-foot squares. Inlaid glass panels on the gun cabinet's double doors displayed a couple dozen long guns, many of them lever guns in various calibers, as well as multiple handguns, including Western-style single-action revolvers.

On the west side of the room, opposite the front door, a three-foot-high spindled wooden handrail jutted out from the front wall, the north wall, and made a right-ninety to join up with the west wall, partitioning off that part of the living room. A gap in the handrail allowed family members and guests to access the sunken section. Dark-red shag carpeting, a loveseat that matched the sofa, two padded straight-back chairs, two small side tables—and a gas fireplace in the northwest corner—created a cozy nook.

Lockhart placed a brown bottle-shaped paper bag on the coffee table, went to the kitchen, then returned with a lowball glass. He blew into the four-ounce glass to clear away some dust then set it beside the paper bag. After laying his Resistol hat on the couch to his left, brim up, he claimed the center cushion and lifted from the paper bag a bottle of Lagavulin 16-year Scotch Whisky. Never having been a drinker, he had asked the guy at the liquor store to give him something that would get him the drunkest the fastest. He had no idea if his wish had been granted, but the guy had had to reach all the way to the top shelf to retrieve this amber-colored specimen Lockhart now held.

Lockhart's late wife had had an awful experience with alcohol growing up. Her parents had been alcoholics, and that had scarred her for life. She had often commented to him; she was glad he was not a drinker. If he had been, she didn't think she could have married him.

Lockhart opened the bottle, filled the lowball glass to the halfway point, then capped the bottle. For the next several seconds, he hovered above the glass, peering at the liquid.

Ever since Jace had been killed, Lockhart had tried everything he could think of to take away his pain. Or even dull the ache, the emptiness in his soul. On multiple occasions, he had chopped wood, bare-chested, in twenty-degree weather until his limbs were numb. That didn't work. But he now had piles of firewood to heat his home for the next five years.

He had sent hundreds, maybe thousands, of rounds of ammunition through his big bore rifles until his left shoulder was left bruised and battered. And that's all he got, a beat-up shoulder.

He had even tried woodworking and whittling, but every project ended with him chucking the piece across the room when it turned out looking nothing like it was supposed to look.

Finally, he had even resorted to going to church more often, reading the Bible, and praying to God, asking God for help, guidance, to give him a sign of what he should do to get back to some semblance of living.

None of it had worked.

His nights were restless. And the sleep he did get was marred by violent images that woke him in a cold sweat. Peace was far from his heart, and what little zest for life he had was slipping away from him with each passing day.

Lockhart raised the glass to eye level and continued his inspection. He knew it was cliché, taking solace in alcohol. But what choice did he have? He had tried everything else he could think of to quell the pain. He sniffed the whisky. There was an aroma there, but it did nothing special for him.

Behind him, the clock above the fireplace, reading half-past six, chimed once.

He brought the glass to his lips and lifted his gaze toward the window, toward the pictures on the sofa table. A framed picture of his wife caught his eye. She was all bundled up in a winter coat, snow falling around her as she looked to the sky, her arms spread wide as the camera had caught her in mid spin.

He spied the whisky, glimpsed the photo, then went back to the spirit. A moment later, he set the glass down and clenched his fists, his twitching forearms resting on his knees. He shut his eyes and gritted his teeth. Then, with a belly roar, he swept everything off the coffee table.

The bottle, the glass, and the spilled liquid lay scattered on the floor, three feet from the front door.

Standing, he raised both arms and flipped over the coffee table.

The table landed on the lounge chairs by the window, sending one sliding to the right.

The sofa table teetered, toppling pictures.

He made a one-eighty and flipped over the sofa before grabbing the cushions and throwing them across the room.

Sidestepping left, he charged the gun cabinet and put his right fist through a glass panel, glass fragments falling onto the floor of the cabinet. Reaching with both hands behind the wooden furniture, he was about to tip it over when he heard a commotion coming from behind him.

• • •

Having been sent into the house by Sierra, his senses picking up fear radiating from his handler, Ranger now barked wildly. The confused dog's woofing vacillated between playful and somewhat businesslike. Clearly, with no bad guy around to bite, he was left waiting and wondering, waiting for a command while wondering about the game Lockhart was playing. More importantly, when was his newfound friend going to let him in on the fun?

Wearing winter boots, blue jeans, and a long winter coat, with the open front door on her right, Sierra stood gaping at the mess. Her gaze settled on Lockhart before it went to the overturned furniture again.

Ranger continued barking.

"Ranger, heel," she said.

The GSD peeled away from Lockhart and sat by her left boot. With his attention alternating from one person to the other, his tongue hanging out as he panted away, he sat waiting for his next command.

Sierra bent over and patted him on the left shoulder. "Settle down, boy. It's okay. Everything's fine. Take it easy." She stood tall to spy Lockhart. "We were almost to your driveway when I saw you getting out of your Jeep and heading into the house."

"You said you were tracking a missing boy and didn't think you'd be here until tomorrow afternoon or the next day."

"Ranger found him sooner than expected."

"How was he, the boy, I mean?"

"A little dehydrated, but alive and well."

"That's good," said Lockhart.

"S0, with the job done," replied Sierra, "I thought I'd show up tonight and surprise you."

He glimpsed the chaotic living room. *Mission*

accomplished.

"But when I rolled up, I heard what sounded like a fight going on in here."

Lockhart ran his left hand through his disheveled hair while stepping away from the gun cabinet.

"So, I got Ranger out of the back and sent him in ahead of me." She glanced around then squinted at the man with a bleeding right hand. She started to ask him a question but ended up stooping to pick up the still-capped bottle of whisky, the empty lowball glass, and a few other things that had been on the coffee table.

"In addition to being a lousy husband and father," he motioned toward the items she held, "turns out I'm lousy at getting drunk, too."

Sierra put the items on the sofa table and faced him. "Don't say that. Their deaths had *nothing* to do with you." She righted the overturned photo frames then struggled to twist the coffee table that was leaning against the lounge chair nearest the door.

He hurried to grab the other half, and together they set it on its legs. Blood from his hand dripped onto the table's surface. He swiped at it with his clean palm.

"Wade, I'm worried about you." She placed the brown paper bag under his bleeding hand and looked him in the eye. "You can't keep going like this. I get it. I know the anger, the rage." She raised a hand. "I'm not trying to compare my abduction and assault to losing a child, but," she shook her head, "I know the frustration of thinking you're not in control.

"Before I adopted Ranger, many times I would wake up in the middle of the night. The sheets were wet. My t-shirt was drenched. And all I could feel was that stinking S.O.B. on top of me." She closed her eyes. *In me.* Sierra waggled her head to dislodge past images before opening her eyes to regard Lockhart. "I'm worried that if you don't find a reason for living, you're going to wind up losing yourself."

She pumped a hand his way. "Now, I know we barely know each other, and our relationship hasn't started off like most relationships do, but if *I'm* not going to be that reason, your *special someone*, then—"

"You're leaving?"

She leaned away from him and frowned. "Wade, I'm right here. I haven't left. I haven't even backed away from you. No, I'm not leaving you. I'm waiting for you to let me help you. You don't have to go through this alone." She laid a flat hand on her chest. "Let me help you."

Lockhart filled his lungs and exhaled, long and slow. "I'm not sure I know how to do that anymore."

She half smiled at him and took his injured hand in hers. "How about we start by you letting me help you with *this*?"

He flexed his hand a couple times, wincing while staring at the glass shard sticking out from between two knuckles. "I feel stupid."

"Don't. No judgement here. I've done similar things

during my own fits. We're only human. We can only take so much." She clutched his forearm and ushered him toward the staircase and the bathroom upstairs. "Come on. Let's get you cleaned up." She motioned toward the stairs. "Ranger, up."

The dog climbed the treads ahead of Lockhart and Sierra.

ONE HOUR LATER

Sierra finished wrapping Lockhart's hand for a second time. After the first time, they had straightened up the living room. Minus the broken glass inside the gun cabinet, everything was now back in order. The exertion, however, had broken open his wound again.

"There." She secured the gauze and set a roll of tape on the handrail. "That should hold up better this time."

He inspected her work. "Thank you."

She took a breath, exhaled, then peered into his eyes. "I meant what I said earlier. This anger isn't good for you." She laid hands on his chest. "You need to find another outlet, a diversion from your pain."

He took her by the upper arms and glanced down. *I've tried.*

She leaned into him and put her right cheek to his sternum. "You need to find something, some*one* to live for. Again, I'm not trying to force myself on you, but—"

The doorbell rang.

Lockhart looked at the front door over the top of Sierra's head.

"Are you expecting someone?" she asked.

"No." He moved her aside and headed for the door while pressing his right elbow against the Ruger Redhawk on his belt. After peeking around the window curtain to see a tiny woman on the front porch, he glanced at the surrounding terrain before opening the door to give the area another inspection. Bad guys often used women to get a homeowner to let his guard down.

"Sheriff Lockhart?"

"Can I help you, Miss?"

"I'm terribly sorry to show up here so late—and without warning." She hoisted a bundle higher up the right side of her waist. "But I was hoping to talk to you."

He squinted at her, the porch light casting a yellowish hue onto her olive-green winter coat, a coat he recalled seeing before. At that time, it was open and nowhere near being big enough to be zipped around its owner's body. He pointed at her. "You were at my son's funeral. You stopped me on the sidewalk."

She nodded. "That was me."

He noted that she now looked even thinner than she had at the funeral. Her jeans were skintight and fit her figure perfectly, along with the winter coat. And her belly bump was now gone.

She struggled to keep the bundle from sliding down to her nonexistent right hip, as a tiny head moved from within the bundle. At the same time, a faint cooing sound was heard.

Lockhart breathed in a burst of cold air before

stepping forward to adjust the material, so that it completely covered the baby. "Forgive me, but their little lungs don't like this bitter air. It's best to keep them completely covered."

She gave him a nervous chuckle. "Thanks. I'm new to all this, and I," a beat, "well, sometimes it," another beat, "it—"

"It can all be a little overwhelming. I know. I've been there."

She smiled.

He poked his chin at her. "What can I do for you?"

She cocked her head at him. "Can we talk? I promise it won't take long, and you can get on with your night."

Lockhart turned sideways and motioned toward the living room. "Would you like to step inside?" He pointed at the baby. "It'll be much better for the little one."

The twenty-year-old woman made a face, glimpsed her child, then came back to the homeowner. "If it's not too much trouble."

"Not at all. Come on in." He stepped inside.

She followed him into the warmth.

He closed the door and shut out the cold.

The woman spotted Sierra and Ranger sitting on the sofa. "I'm so sorry. I had no idea you had company." She spun back toward the door. "I can come back later."

Lockhart raised his left arm to grip her right shoulder. "Miss, you're not interrupting. Now, what did you want to talk to me about?"

The young girl went from Lockhart to Sierra to Lockhart again. "Would it be possible for us to speak in private?" She whipped her head toward Sierra. "No offense, Ma'am."

Sierra smiled then stood. "None taken. Ranger, come." She peeled away from the couch.

Ranger jumped down and followed her.

"We'll be in the den, Wade." Sierra and Ranger walked through the kitchen and disappeared into the next room.

Lockhart faced his guest and arched his brows.

"I'm not sure if you remember or not, but at the funeral I told you I knew Jace from—"

"The Buckin Bronco." Lockhart nodded. "You said he used to come in there, and the two of you would talk."

She smiled. "Yeah. We did. Well," she shifted her baby to her left hip, "I'm not sure how to tell you this, but," she stammered, "well, Jace and I were actually dating."

Lockhart's brows went up again.

She placed a hand on her forehead. "What am I doing? I haven't even told you who I am. I'm Kinsley. Kinsley Harris."

The two shook hands.

"Pleasure to meet you, Miss Harris."

Kinsley sighed and gave him a strained look. "So, Jace never said anything about me?"

"No." Lockhart glanced down. "But that doesn't

surprise me. My son has always held his cards close to the vest. Even when he was in school, he never brought any girls home and never talked about any either. His mother and I respected his privacy."

Biting her lower lip, Kinsley glanced at her baby, then cocked her head at Lockhart, her jaw hanging open a bit.

Lockhart recalled her giving him the same look at the funeral right before she quickly said Jace was a good man and that he'd be missed.

"Sheriff, Jace and I had been," she drew her lips into her mouth before making a face, looking away, then coming back to him, "your son and I were seeing each other *exclusively* for almost a year before he was killed."

The implications of her words hit Lockhart square in the chest like the broad head of a full-grown bison. He eyeballed the newborn then frowned at the baby's mother before doing another back-and-forth, his gaze finishing on her. "You mean..."

Donning an awkward half smile, Kinsley nodded. "This is your grandson."

Lockhart's world spun. His knees went rubbery.

"I wanted so much to tell you at the funeral," her words were spilling out now like water from a firehose, "but you just looked like you had the weight of the world on your shoulders. And I didn't want to add this, too. I'm sorry for not telling you sooner. I really am."

His jaw dropping, Lockhart let out the air his lungs

had been holding. He sniffed and ran fingers across his nose and mouth. After taking a few moments to regain his mental and physical stability, he rubbed his forehead then took another deep breath, exhaling a tick later.

"Would," her voice low, she held her baby a bit higher, "would you like to hold him, Sheriff?"

Lockhart swallowed hard. "May I?"

"Of course." Kinsley leaned forward and extended her arms. "As of last week, he's two months old."

Lockhart cradled his offspring for the next few minutes, his heavy-laden heart lightening with each half spin of his torso as he bounced at the knees ever so slightly.

"I'm not sure if you knew this or not, but," Kinsley came around to stand on Lockhart's right to see her son, "the day before he died, Jace proposed to me. And I accepted."

Lockhart spied her out of the corner of his eye.

"He came up with the idea to tell you the next day. He wanted us to go out for dinner somewhere—"

Lockhart faced her. "Nice."

She met his gaze. "Yeah."

Sighing, Lockhart tipped his head backward and closed his eyes, everything hitting him at once. "That's what he was so excited to tell me about," he mumbled.

"So, he told you...about us, about our son?"

"No. He didn't. He said he had something he wanted to share with me, and that he wanted to do so over dinner," he nodded at Kinsley, "somewhere nice." Lockhart shook his head, his heart getting some closure on his son's final words to him that day.

A minute passed.

Kinsley eyed Lockhart. "Just so you know, Sheriff, I'm not here to get anything out of you."

He eyeballed her. "What do you mean?"

"I'm not looking for any money. I only came here, because I thought you should know," a beat, "that you have a grandson. He has no family alive on my side. My parents were killed in an auto accident when I was fourteen. I spent four years in the foster care system in Michigan before graduating high school and moving out here. I met Jace a year later and—" she waved a hand. "Why am I blabbering on? I'm sorry."

"That's all right."

"Anyway," she spied her boy, "I think Jace would've wanted his father to be part of his son's life," she whipped her head toward Lockhart, "that is, if you *want* to be."

Lockhart smiled at the mother of his grandson. "I do...very much so. Thank you. You have no idea how much this means to me."

Kinsley beamed. "So, you'd like to see him again?"

A tear streaked down a smiling Lockhart's right cheek. "As often as possible."

Another minute went by.

"Do you mind if I use your bathroom? Since giving

birth," Kinsley made a circular motion down by her belly, "my bladder seems to have shrunk."

He rocked his head backward. "Through the kitchen. You can't miss it."

"Thank you so much." Unzipping her coat, she scooted around him, stopped, then turned back. "Are you okay to watch him?"

Lockhart grinned. "Not my first rodeo, Miss. I'll be just fine."

She pointed finger guns at him. "Right. Sorry. Like I said, I'm new to all this." She pivoted. "I'll be right back."

"No hurry." A pulse. "Wait. What's his name?"

"Jace Wade Lockhart."

Lockhart's heart melted, a broad smile growing on his face as he drank in his grandson's face and tiny little fingers. *Jace Wade.*

Thirty seconds later, Lockhart heard the pitter patter of toenails on wood before hearing panting down by his left leg. He glanced down to see Ranger looking up at him. He turned to his left to see a beaming Sierra closing in on him.

"I hope you don't mind, but I couldn't help but overhear everything from the other room." She glanced up and around at all the hard surfaces in the house. "Sound travels far in this place." Her attention went to the baby. "Hi there." Her smile growing wider, she gawked at Jace Wade. "Hi there, you little cutie, you."

"His name is Jace Wade."

She looked up at him, a twinkle in her eye.

"But then," Lockhart nodded, "you would know that, since you heard everything."

Sierra toyed with Jace Wade's tiny hand. "Isn't he just the most precious little thing you've ever seen?"

"I couldn't agree more." He admired his grandson. "You and I are going to be best buds, JW."

She dialed up a quizzical look.

He noticed. "Has a nice ring, doesn't it?"

She smiled. "It does, but you had better run that by momma first."

The two spent the next couple minutes ogling the baby.

Sierra glanced up at Lockhart. Observing a gleam in his eye, she felt her heart flutter. In the next instant, she recalled the prayer she had said before the manhunt for Davis Bronson had gotten underway; specifically, the part where she had asked Jesus to send someone to help Lockhart get on track again, someone who could help him live again. She lifted her eyes toward the ceiling, *Not exactly how I thought You'd answer, Lord*, then inwardly shook her head in amazement. *But then again, Your ways are higher than our ways.* Sierra came back to Lockhart. "Hey, Wade?"

"Yeah?"

"Do you remember when I said you needed to find that special someone to live for?"

He regarded her.

She glimpsed Jace Wade then smiled at Lockhart. "I think you found him."

Lockhart shook his head. "No." He leaned into her and coiled his left arm around her shoulders. "I found a *second* special someone," he said before giving a smiling Sierra a long kiss on the lips.

— Thank You —

Thank you for purchasing and reading *AMBUSH*. I hope you enjoyed this second installment in the BIG SKY series of modern sheriff crime thrillers. But the ride's not over yet. Keep reading for a sneak peek at the third book, *RECKONING*.

As for yours truly, I'm hard at work, writing my next novel. So, until we meet again...

Blessings and Peace,

Alex

P.S. Remember to get your FREE ebook, *Escape & Evade*, at my website (AlexAnderNovelist.com).

Excerpt from RECKONING

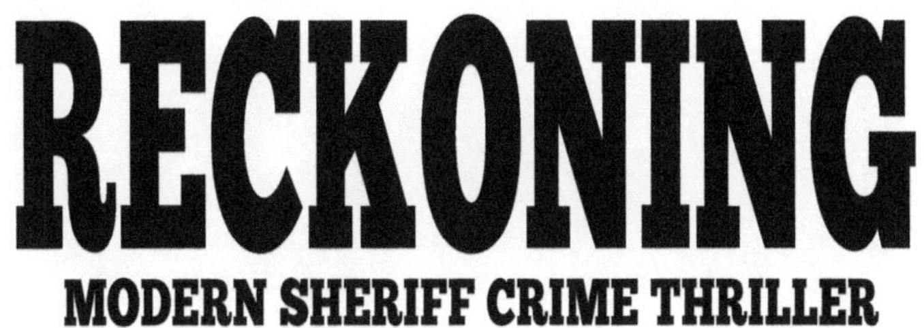

ALEX
ANDER

CHAPTER 1
LEVER GUNS & CAR SEATS

15 JANUARY—8:53 A.M.
BIG SKY COUNTY
WYATT, MONTANA

It wasn't even halfway through January, and every day of the month had seen snowfall in Big Sky County. Some days brought several inches, while other days saw only a dusting or flurries. In addition to the white stuff collecting on roadways and sidewalks and being shoveled into piles everywhere, the temperatures had been colder than normal. Low twenties had been the daytime highs with most nights seeing single digits on average. Hardened county residents, many of whom had lived in Big Sky their whole lives, hadn't experienced weather this cold and snowy in a long time.

Its windshield wipers going, clearing away what seemed like a constant snowfall, the boxy, old-style hunter-green Jeep Grand Wagoneer, wood-grained panels on its sides and tailgate, rolled over the freshly deposited three inches of snow, bypassing citizens of Wyatt, Montana, who were making their way from one warm building to another or to their vehicles. Most people had their hands full or were snuggling up to whoever was with them, each person shielding the other from a bitter wind. Those unlucky enough to be traveling solo just put their heads down and speed walked to their destination.

Inside the Grand Wagoneer, 45-year-old Big Sky County Sheriff Wade Lockhart spun the steering wheel to the right and navigated the SUV into a parking spot across from the sheriff's office.

Located on Main Street, in the center of Wyatt, the redbrick building had once been a post office. Then, after a gun store had occupied the structure for a few years, it became available again after the firearm business had gone bankrupt. Now, for the past six months, it had been the new headquarters for the Big Sky Sheriff's Office.

Lockhart shut off the engine, climbed out, and opened the right rear door. After spending the next few minutes hunched over and fiddling with something, he backed out and slung a lever action rifle over his left shoulder, muzzle pointing upward.

"Hi, Sheriff."

Lockhart turned to see one of Big Sky's newest residents, Kristina Walters. The two had crossed paths back in October when he had been investigating his son Jace's murder. Lockhart recalled his first meeting with the twenty-eight-year-old, five-nothing slender woman who, at that time, had been working as a hooker, and as a dancer at a strip club in Roseburg, Idaho. Her face had sported every imaginable kind of makeup known to mankind—mascara, rouge, eyeliner, eye shadow, lipstick, all of it.

     Excerpt from RECKONING

Now he saw a woman who had traded in her face paint, miniskirts, and five-inch spiked heels for—he gave her outfit a quick peek—for ankle-high black winter boots, blue jeans, a long dark-gray winter coat, and what looked like a hand-knitted red stocking cap. Her long, black curly hair stuck out from under the covering. *Yup,* he thought. *A real Montanan.* "Tina," he replied. Since moving to Montana, she had started going by 'Tina.' *A new start deserves a new name,* she had told him.

"I can't believe how cold it is here," she said.

He eyeballed her rosy cheeks, thin face, brown eyes, and long lashes, lashes that appeared to have a modest amount of mascara on them. He thought of his deceased wife. Outside of a light layer of mascara, Cheryl had never worn makeup a day in her life, at least never in all the days he had known her. *I'm a natural beauty,* she had joked.

Lockhart thought of Sierra, his girlfriend. She too hadn't worn any makeup in the short time the two had been together. Perhaps that was what had caught his eye when he first met her. Whether or not he knew it, he had always been attracted to women who didn't cover up their faces but let their true nature shine. Inwardly shaking his head to drag himself away from the mental sidebar his thoughts had gone down, he focused on Tina. "Yes, it's definitely been a cold one." He poked his chin at her. "How are you settling in here? How's the job going?"

Through his undersheriff, Lockhart had discovered

Tina had worked as a vet assistant and had been going to school to become a veterinary technician before her life fell apart, and she soon found herself stripping and hooking to pay the bills. He hadn't been told the entire story about what had happened to her; however, his undersheriff had said something about Tina being shunned by her parents, by her religion. But he didn't need to know the gritty details to know he wanted to help her. So, he had acted, serving as a liaison between Tina and Big Sky's only veterinarian, a man who had been searching for someone to help him with the mundane chores around the clinic: administering medication, bathing animals, collecting samples, cleaning the facilities, tasks like that.

Lockhart had paid Tina's travel expenses and set her up in a motel, so she could get a feel for Wyatt, see if the town was a good fit for her. During her stay, she had interviewed with the veterinarian and was offered the job. The pay wasn't great, but she had a little money saved up. Between her savings, a two-week advance on her salary, and a promise from Lockhart that he'd kick in some financial help if she needed it, Tina had decided to make the jump and move to Wyatt, Montana.

"The job is great," said a beaming Tina. "I love working with animals again. There're no lies, no deceit with them. You know exactly what you're getting." She reached out and squeezed his forearm. "I can't thank you enough for everything you've done for me, Sheriff,

     Excerpt from RECKONING

getting me this job, helping me move here."

He raised a hand. "I may have greased the wheels, but you still had to put in the hard work."

"I know, but if you hadn't knocked on my door that night, I'd still be," she stopped short, "well, you know what I'd still be doing."

· "That's all in the past." He gave Wyatt a glance then came back to her. "You're one of us now. We take care of our own."

She pointed at him. "That reminds me. I have some money for you, but," she made a face, "I'm afraid I left it at home."

Lockhart had paid the deposit and part of her first month's rent payment. He waved her off. "Don't worry about it."

"That's the thing. I *do* worry about it. I pay my debts," she smiled again, "especially to those who've done so much for me."

He regarded her bright, cheery, youthful countenance. *She looks so much younger without all that junk on her face.* "I'm just glad I could help."

Tina checked her watch. "I have to get to work, but," she faced him, "if you're going to be around this afternoon, I could get the money during my lunch hour and drop it off to you."

"That would be fine, but really," he pumped a hand her way, "there's no rush."

She wiped a gloved hand over her face, to clear away

some snow, then pressed her lips together and gave him a long, tender look. "You're one of the nicest men I know, you know that?"

"Thank you."

She came in for a quick hug then backed away. "Okay, well...I better let you go." She waved, "Bye, Sheriff," then continued down the sidewalk toward the clinic.

He watched her leave, inwardly pleased she was getting her life on track again. *God be praised.* He retrieved a car seat from the Jeep, shut the door with his foot, and strolled around the right-front bumper, his lever gun still hanging off his left shoulder. Holding the small car seat in his right hand, a thick blanket completely covering the portable seat, the six-one, one-sixty Lockhart looked like he was getting ready to do a bicep curl as he stepped off the sidewalk. He paused and frowned. *God be praised?* He glanced down. *When have I ever thought that before?*

Moments later, he shook his head and hurried across the street. His black Ariat pull-on work boots crunched snow underfoot. His black Resistol fur felt cattleman-crown cowboy hat and black mid-thigh leather fringe jacket—with all the fringe having been cut off immediately after purchase—were gathering a layer of tiny snowflakes. Blue jeans rounded out his attire.

An oncoming truck slowed.

Lockhart pulled up.

          Excerpt from RECKONING

An arm emerged from behind the driver's rolled-down window, and a man waved, then motioned.

Lockhart waved back then crossed the street. Passing through two sets of double doors, he entered the empty main lobby of the sheriff's office. Black leather chairs sat side by side on the walls to the left and right. Among the chairs, several two-foot-square low tables were strategically placed to allow visitors to set beverages or other items down. Overhead, tube lighting cast a bright 5000 Kelvin hue over the entire area. Gray tile floors throughout met up with small, carpeted sections where the chairs and tables were.

Lockhart strolled down the tiled 'runway' to a four-foot-high redbrick wall that bisected the lobby from administration and the deputies' cubicles. Above the wall, glass rose to the ten-foot-high, tiled ceiling. Two, five-by-two-foot dark oak wooden saloon doors were positioned at the brick wall's horizontal halfway point, a foot off the floor and right in line with the front doors.

He pushed on the left door and walked into the admin section, leading with the car seat.

The door swung by the other one, swung back inside, then repeated the process a couple times before settling.

Seated at her desk on the right, right next to the brick wall, 38-year-old Bristol Mackenzie looked up, a headset arched over her long blonde hair pulled up into a messy bun. She wore light-red rectangular eyeglasses that matched the red ribbon holding her hair up. Cocking her head and frowning at the 'package' her boss was carrying, she spoke into the boom microphone that ran from the headset to her mouth. "Yes, we need them delivered sooner rather than later."

On his twelve o'clock, just outside the door to his office on the left, 35-year-old Piper Jennings pecked away at her computer.

"Morning, Piper," he said.

She shot him a quick look then went back to her task. "Good morning, W—" she did a double-take at the 'package' he was carrying before her brows came together, "ade."

Lockhart ducked into his office.

Dressed in blue jeans, a tan-colored official uniform shirt, sleeves rolled up to her elbows, the five-six, 125-pound undersheriff stood and pointed brown cowboy boots toward Lockhart's open office. Plopping hands onto the gun belt that held her Glock 19, magazine pouches, two-way radio, handcuffs, and other tools of her trade, she turned toward Bristol, her scowl deepening.

The two women exchanged similar expressions.

"Thank you. I appreciate you looking into this," said Bristol before tapping her headset a moment later while marching toward Piper.

Sporting straight, shoulder-length dirty blonde hair, blue eyes, a narrow, slightly upturned nose, prominent chin, and a beauty mark an inch from the right corner of her wide-lipped mouth, Piper ambled into the sheriff's

     Excerpt from RECKONING

office.

Two beats later, showing off black jeans, red faux snakeskin square-toed cowboy boots, and a white blouse, Bristol arrived to stand on Piper's right. Both women watched Lockhart pull back a blanket and extract a baby from the car seat.

Half grinning, he sat in his chair, crossed his legs, ankle on knee, and cradled the baby in his lap.

The women gave each other another look before Piper opened her mouth to show off white teeth, a noticeable gap between her two upper front teeth. "Um," she folded her arms across her chest, "help me out here, Wade. The math isn't adding up. You and Sierra have only been seeing each other for a couple of months now, so-o-o," she held out her hands, palms up, "is there something you want to tell us?"

He frowned while looking away from the women, pretending to be thinking. "No, I," he paused, "I don't think so. Oh, wait." He dipped his forehead toward the rifle on the other side of his desk. "I did want to ask if you'd clean my Henry there. I put some rounds through it yesterday and haven't had time to clean it yet."

Simultaneously, Piper and Bristol made a show of crossing their arms in front of them while each cocked her head at him.

Following another five seconds of keeping a straight face, he smiled, "Oh, you're wondering about," he held up the baby, "*this* young man." He spent the next minute giving them a shortened version of what had happened, then finished with, "His name is Jace Wade Lockhart."

Both women looked on, their mouths hanging open. A tick later, after recovering, they raced toward Lockhart's desk, Piper pulling into the lead at the last moment.

Thinking he had seen an elbow or two thrown, he smiled inwardly before motioning toward his Henry. "The gun's right there, Piper."

"Clean your own rifle." She reached out with both hands. "Gimme. Gimme. I want baby."

Chuckling, he forfeited his grandson.

"Ooh," Piper cooed. "You are such a beautiful thing. You know that?" She bounced slightly while rocking Jace Wade. "Oh, I can see your daddy's sparkling blue eyes." She did a one-eighty and headed for the doorway. "You're going to be a heartbreaker, too, aren't you?"

"So, you're not going to clean my rifle?" asked Lockhart.

Piper cranked her head around. "You *know* I'll clean it," she went back to Jace Wade, "right after I've had my fill of baby." She pretended to take a couple bites of the infant. "You're so delicious. I'm going to eat you up. Yes, I am." She waggled her head at the boy. "Yes, I am."

"Don't go too far with him, Piper," said Bristol. "I'm next."

"Catch me if you can," retorted the undersheriff while leaving Lockhart's office.

Bristol shook her head then turned back toward a smiling Lockhart. She took in his short, light-brown hair, sky-blue eyes, and long eyelashes.

He noticed her grinning at him, her head tipped to one side as she held the tip of one of her eyeglasses' temples inside pursed lips. "What?" he said.

"I haven't seen you like this since before," becoming stoic, she hesitated, glanced down, then faced him again, her pleased countenance returning. "It's good to see you smiling again, Wade."

He nodded. "Thanks, Bristol."

"I realize things still have to be pretty fresh, but," she rocked her head backward, "I'm sure he's going to be a real blessing in your life. I'm really glad you have him."

Lockhart eyed the doorway, his ears picking up a cooing Piper outside. "So am I." A moment. "So am I."

"Well," his secretary put her spectacles back on, "before I go cut in out there, I wanted to tell you that that lawyer called for you again this morning." The attorney had called three times yesterday. Each time, Lockhart had told Bristol to tell him he wasn't in. "Thankfully, this time," continued Bristol, "I could *honestly* say you weren't in."

He nodded.

"The guy's just going to keep calling, Wade. Those people don't give up."

"Battle of wills, I guess."

She rolled her eyes. "And knowing how strong *your*

will is," a beat, "I'll be lying to him until his client is put to death."

He curled up one side of his mouth. "At least you know there's an end in sight."

• • •

For the last five minutes, Piper had fielded incoming calls for Bristol, so the latter woman could hold the baby.

"Thank you for watching him overnight," said Kinsley. At a hundred pounds, 20-year-old Kinsley Harris had a skinny, five-one build. She had long black straight hair with straight bangs down to her thin eyebrows. Her pale white skin was speckled with brown freckles on her cheeks and nose, and she had a smallish head, petite chin, and narrow lips. "I can't tell you how good it felt to get a full night's sleep. I hope he was good for you."

"He fussed for a bit," replied Lockhart, "but Jace used to do the same thing at that age. His mother would sing him this song while I rubbed his belly." Lockhart barely shook his head. "Didn't take long, and he was sleeping peacefully."

Smiling at the story, Kinsley cocked her head at Lockhart. "You'll have to teach me that song."

"I was never the singing type. That was all Cheryl."

Kinsley pressed her lips together then nodded abruptly. "I should probably get going. JW has a checkup later this morning."

"Well," Bristol handed off the baby, "if you ever need a sitter, all you have to do is ask."

"That goes for me, too," said Piper, stepping away from the front desk and approaching the gathering. She beamed at the baby. "I'd watch you anytime." Her eyes big, she gave Jace Wade a broad, toothy smile. "Yes, I would, you sweet little thing you."

Kinsley placed Jace Wade in the car seat and wrapped him in the blanket. "Well, if my," she stood tall and regarded Lockhart, "semi," she tilted her head at the man, "sort of...father-in-law says it's okay," her brows up, she studied him.

Lockhart looked up from the car seat to meet Kinsley's gaze. He nodded, "I trust them," then went back to gazing at his grandson.

Kinsley's shoulders drooped a bit, and she lost some of her radiance.

Bristol's eyes shifted from the girl to her boss to the girl again.

Recovering, Kinsley picked up the car seat, covered Jace Wade with another blanket, and gave the women a crisp, forced smile. "Thank you for the offer. I might just take you up on that." A beat. "It was nice meeting you both."

Bristol: "You too."

Piper: "Likewise."

Kinsley faced Lockhart and raised a tentative hand. "Bye, Sheriff."

He nodded once. "Drive safely."

"I will." She pushed her way through the saloon doors and entered the cold weather a few steps later.

A grinning Piper slapped Lockhart on the arm on her way toward his office. "I better see to cleaning that rifle of yours."

"Thanks, Piper." He gaped through all the glass windows between him and Main Street, his eyes on the car seat, as Kinsley skirted across the street and made a left, leaving his vision a second later.

"Wade, you do know that girl's reaching out to you, right?" said Bristol.

Lockhart faced his secretary, his brows inching closer together.

"Didn't you see her heart sink when you didn't respond to her father-in-law comment?"

He scratched his chin while turning his head to squint at the street outside.

"Now, I don't know her family situation," continued Bristol, "but it was clear she's definitely trying to find out where she stands with *you*."

"She did mention she spent four years in foster care after her parents died. And that JW has no one alive on *her* side of the family."

A frustrated Bristol looked at the ceiling while pumping open hands in the air before backhanding him in the upper arm. "See? That poor girl is all alone in the world with a newborn baby. She's probably scared out of her wits, trying to figure out how she's going to do everything all by herself."

Lockhart came back to Bristol. "She's the mother of my grandson and someone who was obviously important to Jace. Of course, she can count on me to help her out."

"Have you *said* that to her?"

He half closed one eye at the street again.

Bristol raised a corner of her mouth and shook her head at him. "You're so much like my father. He, too, had a heart of gold. He'd do anything for us kids, but to have a heartfelt conversation with the man? Nope. Wasn't going to happen. Eventually, my siblings and I realized what he *said* wasn't what mattered. What mattered was what he *did*."

Lockhart chewed over her words. She wasn't all that far off. There were only two people he had ever opened up to—his mother and his wife. They were gone now, though. And on some level, they had taken with them his desire to share feelings with anyone else. Plus, let's face it. He was a man, and most men didn't share feelings. Lockhart squinted. *This one didn't, anyway.*

"Look," resumed Bristol, "all I'm—"

A phone rang.

She shot a glance toward her desk then started backing away from Lockhart. "You're a bright guy, Wade. Pay attention to the signs, and you'll see what I'm seeing." Bristol turned her back on him while tapping her headset. "Sheriff's Office. Big Sky County. Bristol speaking."

Lockhart folded arms across his chest, cupping his right elbow while stroking his chin with his right hand. Bristol's words played again in his mind. *She's definitely trying to find out where she stands with you.*

"Let me see if he's in," said Bristol before she tapped her headset and eyed her boss. "Wade, it's that lawyer guy."

He spied his secretary.

She cocked her head at him while arching her brows. It was a classic 'what do you want me to do?' look.

But the sheriff side of him saw something entirely different in her eyes. They were pleading with him to take the call, to save her from having to play gatekeeper. He ran his tongue over his lower teeth a few times, grimaced, then jerked his head toward his office, "Send him to me," before he strolled toward his workplace, rubbing the back of his neck.

Bristol's voice: "You're in luck, sir. He's in. I'm transferring you now."

• • •

Five Minutes Later...

While putting on his leather jacket, Lockhart marched out of his office. "Bristol?"

She faced him.

"Push my morning appointments to the afternoon."

     Excerpt from RECKONING

He flattened his coat's collar. "If I need to cancel them later, I'll call."

"Um," she sat upright in her chair, "okay." A tick. "Where are you off to in such a hurry?"

Sticking out an arm ahead of him, "To meet with my son's murderer," he barged through the saloon doors.

www.ingramcontent.com/pod-product-compliance
Lightning Source LLC
Chambersburg PA
CBHW021353150726
47989CB00005B/2230